GAMES FOR LOVERS

Ryan Craig

GAMES FOR LOVERS

OBERON BOOKS
LONDON

WWW.OBERONBOOKS.COM

First published in 2019 by Oberon Books Ltd
521 Caledonian Road, London N7 9RH
Tel: +44 (0) 20 7607 3637 / Fax: +44 (0) 20 7607 3629
e-mail: info@oberonbooks.com
www.oberonbooks.com

A catalogue record for this book is available from the British Library.

PB ISBN: 9781786828194
E ISBN: 9781786828170

Printed and bound by 4EDGE Limited, Hockley, Essex, UK.
eBook conversion by Lapiz Digital Services, India.

10 9 8 7 6 5 4 3 2 1

Author's Note

I'd like to thank some of the people who've helped bring the play into being; Ria Parry, Dom Coyote, Alexandra Maher, Ross Armstrong, Harry Melling, Jess Murphy, Jemima Rooper, Allen Leech, Nick Blood, Kara Tointon, Antonia Kinlay, Luke Norris, Helen George, and Arthur Darville. Also Rose Cobbe, Sebastian Born, Laura Collier, Anthony Banks, James Seabright, Nica Burns, and Emma Brunjes.

RC London, July 2019.

Games for Lovers was first performed at The Vaults, London on 12 July 2019 with the following cast:

LOGAN	Calum Callaghan
MARTHA	Evanna Lynch
JENNY	Tessie Orange-Turner
DARREN	Billy Postlethwaite

Creative Team
Director, Anthony Banks
Set Designer, Simon Scullion
Costume Designer, Susan Kulkarni
Lighting Designer, Matt Haskins
Composition and Sound Designers, Ben and Max Ringham
Movement Director, Nathan M. Wright
Casting Director, Danielle Tarento

Production Team
Company Stage Manager, Ruth Burgon
Production Manager, Ben Arkell
Producer, James Seabright
Associate Producer & General Manager, Johnny Wood
Line Producer, Jennifer Davis
Development Coordinator, Debbie Morris
Production Coordinator, Luke Gledsdale
Assistant Producer (Stage One Trainee), Lottie Bauer
Press Representative, Kevin Wilson

Act One

MARTHA, DARREN, JENNY and LOGAN address the audience.

MARTHA: Have I had any disastrous relationships? Oh yes. Most of them.

LOGAN: Love? Load of bollocks really isn't it?

MARTHA: Actually now I come to think of it, all of them.

JENNY: God yeah, shit loads. My love life is a total clusterfuck. Whose isn't?

DARREN: Me? None. Way I see it, I never get rejected, I just find out whether the chick has good taste.

MARTHA: There was this one lad called Orpheus. Whole relationship was a shambles. Then he dumps me on a group Whatsapp.

DARREN: Look the world isn't "one woman one vote" yeah. If she turns you inside out it doesn't mean you've been done over by the whole of woman-kind. It's just one person's opinion. Yeah? So really I don't sweat it.

MARTHA: Two days later Orpheus begs me to come to Christmas at his parents' house. Pretend we're still together. Said they were big fans of mine and it would really upset them if they knew we were finished.

JENNY: I met this nutcase on Tinder.

MARTHA: I went. I felt bad for them. They did call their son Orpheus.

JENNY: First thing he says when we meet is "I haven't eaten for three days." I said "why on earth haven't you eaten for

1

three days?" He says "I was nervous about our date."
I said "what, really?" He said "I've read so much about
you, you sound awesome." I said "hold on, what d'you
mean you've read all about me?" He says. "You know,
all your tweets and that, all your Facebook posts.
Everything." At that point I should really've fled.

MARTHA: I had to get off those apps. For about three weeks
last year I saw this guy Aiden. I could tell he was a player,
he was always checking his phone. Finally, he told me
he couldn't see a future, and ended it. Then, like, six
months later I get this message ...Hey Martha916, your
profile looks really interesting, I'd love to get to know you.
Drink? Aiden. Am I really that forgettable?

JENNY: ...anyway he sat there, this guy, all night, talking
endlessly about his cat, who he was sure was dying of
tuberculosis, and at the end of the meal, which he scoffed
at high speed by the way, at the end of this incredibly
awkward meal he says to me; "look I'm a bit skint just
now, d'you think you could stump for the bill? I'll get it
next time." "*Next time*?!"

MARTHA: Once I wanted to end it with this guy Will. Will
was really fragile, you know, terribly sensitive, so I got
myself all worked up, you know...

DARREN: Am I in a relationship right now?

LOGAN: Sorry, is that strictly relevant?

DARREN: Let me answer that by saying this.

MARTHA: And just before I'm about to end it, Will says,
"Big news! I got this amazing job offer. In Los Angeles!
But it would mean us breaking up and that would make
me sad." I said "oh...no...that's...brilliant...but also...
awful." And he said "awful? Really?" And I said "yes...
yes it would break my heart if you left and went all that

2

way. I'd be devastated." I really spread it on thick, you know, told him how shattered I'd be if he left, but all the while in my head I'm jumping up and down, screaming "Yes! Yes! Thank You God! I never have to see this loser again." And then he says. "Fuck it then, I won't go." And I say: "what's that now?" And he says, "obviously we mean too much to each other. Even if *I* could cope with the separation, I simply can't do it to you. You're too fragile." So I said "what about this fantastic, once in a lifetime job opportunity" and he says, listen to this one, he says; "I will forgo it to be with you." And I said…"yippee!" And we hugged. Then I threw up.

DARREN: I work in the city. In *risk*. Sharp end shit. Long hours, so the love life has to be carefully strategized.

LOGAN: I am…*seeing* someone.

JENNY: It's early days. I don't wanna…

LOGAN: Sorry, did I sound hesitant?

DARREN: You know. I go out…have *a hell of a lot of fun*…

JENNY: Job's ok. Web site design. Is it what I want to be doing?

DARREN: I have a lot of modern, urban relationships sue me.

JENNY: I went to St Martin's, fine art, didn't finish. My tutor said I had nothing new to say. Said my work was clichéd. Then he tried to shag me.

MARTHA: Am I anxious about meeting someone?

DARREN: I've got zero anxiety about meeting someone.

MARTHA: Incredibly anxious. Who isn't?

DARREN: One. I've got the swagger. Two. I've got the chat.

3

LOGAN: Dating's a pretty fraught sort of lark isn't it.

DARREN: You want to succeed out there, you gotta be armed to the teeth with chat.

MARTHA: Mum and Dad are anxious for me. They'd like me to marry to a nice dentist like my sister.

DARREN: It's a numbers game, right? Take the knock-backs on the chin, get up of the mat. Live to fight another…

JENNY: Mum paints postcards for tourists.

DARREN: This is a contest.

JENNY: Cornwall coast mainly.

DARREN: This is a bout. You're in the ring getting pounded over and over.

MARTHA: They don't say anything, but I can tell they're disappointed.

DARREN: …so you never…never…show your vulnerabilities. Once they smell the fear, you're finished. They tear you to pieces.

LOGAN: Grew up on a farm. Not a working farm, I wasn't… *milking*.

DARREN: Sorry, do I seem defensive?

JENNY: My Dad? Hugely charismatic. Devoured life. Mended boats.

DARREN: What d'you wanna hear? That I had a bad relationship with my mum, so I don't let women get too close? Wrong. Me and mum get on great. She's my pal. Speak to her every day. I'm her wonderboy chuckle bucket.

JENNY: Really loved his work, dedicated to those boats.

DARREN: ...I think I may've overshared just then, sorry.

JENNY: He'd spend days holed up that shed. Named me after the one he was fixing when I was born. Jenny.

LOGAN: Name's Logan. Mr. Matthews to you. Teach PE at a boys' school. Bloody buggers. Naah...they're a good bunch really.

JENNY: When Dad left I went off the rails for a bit.

DARREN: My Dad though? This guy. My twelfth birthday he takes me to Macdonald's. Drive thru, off the A forty-six. Got me a Happy Meal, went outside to take a call. Never saw him again. That's Dad.

LOGAN: Dad never said much. Mum neither.

DARREN: Mum had to drive all the way out to Stroud. Pick me up. This snivelling wretch of a kid standing on the lay-by, sucking pop from a straw. She was livid.

LOGAN: I never thought of him as ...unhappy.

DARREN: But, look, you know, I don't dwell. I don't dwell on that stuff. The negative. I stay positive. Always positive, always looking ahead.

LOGAN: So it was odd when he jumped in front of that bus.

DARREN: Catz. Darren Catz. Sometimes, to keep things interesting, I go by a fun pseudonym like The Cat. Tom Cat. Catch of the day. Wham.

MARTHA: Martha Wiggly. Single.

DARREN: Important to project an aura of devil-may-care. Like I'll wear an eye-catching hat, a pair of funky trousers. Stand out from the crowd.

MARTHA: There is...actually... someone I like...

DARREN: No I'm not afraid to look like a clown.

MARTHA: Thing is we've known each other practically our whole lives. So it's...you know...

DARREN: We all wear different masks,

MARTHA: Awkward.

DARREN: We all play different roles ... online profiles, job interviews, social gatherings, everyone's competing for attention, you got to give yourself an edge. I will not apologise for that. But I never *use* people, I'm way too "woke" for that. I'm beyond "woke". I've transcended "woke". I have evolved to the next level of being, I'm playing on a whole new stratosphere

JENNY: Am I anxious about meeting someone?

MARTHA: I'd never act on it, no.

JENNY: I think I'm more anxious about driving them away.

MARTHA: I'd never ruin such a long-standing friendship by telling him. Anyway the moment's gone now...

DARREN: Rule number one. Grasp the moment or it's gone forever. You've got thirty seconds...less. A brief window in which to make a lasting impact.

MARTHA: Actually I might tell him. Tonight. I'll tell him tonight. What's the worst that could happen?

DARREN: So we're in this bar...

Bell rings.

GAME TWO – BOSTON CRAB

Bar. A sudden burst of laughter as DARREN and LOGAN spot each other across the room.

LOGAN: Dazza! Is that you?

DARREN: Hello mate.

LOGAN: Boston Crab!

BOTH: Dive!

> *They throw themselves into crab like formation wrestling clinch. It is supposed to be a bit of fun, but there is, underneath, an element of serious competitiveness. LOGAN gets the better of DARREN and pins him to ground.*

LOGAN: How long's it been?

DARREN: Not long enough. *(Laughs.)*

LOGAN: Funny. Yield?!

DARREN: I'll tell you what is funny. You look like shit.

LOGAN: That is funny. Coming from you. Now *yield!*

> *LOGAN presses DARREN down harder.*

DARREN: *Never!*

> *With great physical effort LOGAN rolls himself out of the headlock and gets DARREN in one.*

LOGAN: You never could beat me at this. *(Presses down harder.)*

DARREN: Aah! You fucker.

LOGAN: Yield?!

DARREN: Never!

LOGAN: Say Logan is the King.

DARREN: I can't.

LOGAN: Say Logan is the King.

DARREN: I just had a hip operation you dick.

LOGAN: Oh. Shit. Sorry.

> *LOGAN releases as grip, but as he does, DARREN seizes the opportunity and rolls him over, pinning him down.*

LOGAN: Oi!

DARREN: First rule of Boston Crab. Never lower your guard.

LOGAN: Sneaky bastard!

DARREN: Yield?!

LOGAN: Fuck no! Never!

> *With great physical effort LOGAN, rolls them both over and pins DARREN down.*

LOGAN: Give up now?

DARREN: I'm actually enjoying this.

> *They both suddenly feel very awkward.*

LOGAN: People watching?

DARREN: Yeah. We'd better…

LOGAN: Yeah.

> *LOGAN releases DARREN, they get up. Stand looking at each other, smiling awkwardly.*

DARREN: Anyway. It's…uh…s'good to see you.

LOGAN: Yeah. I miss you. Dick.

DARREN: I miss you too. Cock.

Beat. They smile.

LOGAN: So what you doing in this gaff?

DARREN: Sharking. What else? On the lookout.:

LOGAN: Best of British mate. I never knew anyone more
hopeless with the ladies.

DARREN: I'm not the dude you knew at college buddy.

LOGAN: Who was that one you were with?

DARREN: There've been so many.

LOGAN: Nina. Was it? Nina Collins.

DARREN: I don't…Was it? I don't…

LOGAN: Christ, she really did a number on you didn't she?

DARREN: Honestly, I can hardly remember.

LOGAN: I mean she wiped the walls with you mate.

DARREN: Like I say, another lifetime. I don't think about her,
I don't think about her, what she did, what she…did, my
eyes are facing forwards, ok? Like a raptor.

LOGAN: You remember that mustard tank top you used
to wear…

DARREN: Fuck.

LOGAN: And those…on your feet. *Clogs*…you really were the
biggest dork.

DARREN: Found my mojo since then.

LOGAN: I mean a good-looking chick came along your jaw
went to jelly.

DARREN: And that's another thing. I don't refer to women
as chicks.

9

LOGAN: You're right. Inappropriate. Sorry.

DARREN: I call them "targets".

LOGAN: What?!

DARREN: Got to respect the enemy.

LOGAN: Hang on…

DARREN: This is a war. This is a contest. Show the slightest weakness, you get pummelled.

LOGAN: Jesus, what happened to you?

DARREN: I woke up! That's what happened. I found my mojo, became *the captain of my own destiny.*

LOGAN: Did you join a cult?

DARREN: …night after night I stood in bars like this, exactly like this, and observed. Human interaction, social intercourse… and I realised something: Sensitive guys. Woman aren't interested. Beta males, forget it. A woman doesn't want some needy little house-pet shuffling along after them, his balls in his hands, they want a Colonel. A Tsar. Someone who takes life by the throat, who lives by his own rules, a *buccaneer*, who bends the system to his will.

LOGAN: But aren't you making a wildly sweeping generalisation?

DARREN: Oh Logan. Logan, Logan, Logan. My poor, deluded, yokel friend. I bet if I sent you in-field unprepared you'd come out with some naff opener, like "hey, like your frock."

LOGAN: Women like to be complimented, don't they?

DARREN: Wrong.

LOGAN: Wrong?

DARREN: My compliments are never, *never* given away for free. They have to earn it. Right? Now...once you're in, once you're chatting, you can plant a subliminal message. I'll say "yes, yes, that's very interesting, and I can tell that..." and then I'll touch their arm...ever so slightly... like this and I'll say... "I can tell that you... *like me...*" *(Touches LOGAN's arm.)* "...don't suffer fools." See? *(Touches his arm again.)* You like me. Neuro-linguistic programming.

LOGAN: I don't believe this.

DARREN: Told you...I changed. I even tell then my name's Wham.

LOGAN: Wham?

DARREN: Say your name's Darren it's a conversation killer. But say you're called Wham. You've got something interesting to talk about.

LOGAN: And you've got something interesting to talk about have you?

DARREN: Course not. That's why I have a number of carefully rehearsed routines.

MARTHA appears on the other side of the bar.

LOGAN: All right. Show me.

DARREN: Show you?

LOGAN: Why not?

DARREN: ... it's early ...very poor woman-flow...

LOGAN: What about her? At the bar.

DARREN: Christ. All right. Christ.

11

LOGAN: Unless you want to bottle it.

DARREN: Fine. Fine. But keep focussed, I'm gonna be changing gears all over the place.

LOGAN: Don't worry, I'll be watching very closely.

DARREN adopts a swagger, and approaches MARTHA.

DARREN: Hi babe, so what do you do for fun?

MARTHA: Oh God.

DARREN: Nope. Name's Wham. And you are?

MARTHA: Waiting for my boyfriend. So…if you don't mind…

DARREN: Sounds like a riot, can I join in?

MARTHA: Better if you didn't.

DARREN: Why? You got a contagious disease? *(Laughs.)*.

MARTHA: More of an allergy. To slimy men in bars.

DARREN: I can tell that you *(Touches her arm.)* like me…don't suffer fools…

MARTHA: What are you doing, never touch me.

DARREN: Ok…

MARTHA: OK?

DARREN: Ok…

MARTHA: Ok?

DARREN: Ok. Yes. Sorry.

DARREN looks over to LOGAN. LOGAN puts his thumbs up. DARREN tries again.

DARREN: Tell you what. Take a quick quiz with me and I'll walk away.

MARTHA: Thanks, but no.

DARREN: Come on, it's easy, I ask five really basic questions. Twist is; you have to give the wrong answers. Pull it off and I buy you a drink and never bother you again.

MARTHA: That last bit's tempting.

DARREN: Hmm, yeah…Nah…You're not ready for this.

MARTHA: Not ready? For your inane quiz?

DARREN: You need a bit of edge. A bit of street smarts for this, but you seem a bit…I wouldn't wanna take advantage.

MARTHA: Seem a bit what?

DARREN: I don't mean to be rude. Simple.

MARTHA: Are you daring me? Is that what you're doing?

DARREN: I'm happy to shake hands and walk away right now, no hard feelings.

He puts his hand out. She ignores it.

MARTHA: All I have to do is answer the questions wrong?

DARREN: And I buy you a beverage of your choice, yes.

MARTHA: And never bother me again, don't forget that part.

DARREN: And never bother you again.

MARTHA: And if I lose?

DARREN: You have to give me your name.

MARTHA: That's all?

DARREN: And your phone number. Can't say fairer than that.

MARTHA: Hang on my phone number?

DARREN: Ok. I knew you weren't ready for this...

MARTHA: Fine. Go on then. Ask me your stupid questions. Go.

DARREN: Ok. Ready? Question one. What's your name?

MARTHA: Boutros Boutros Ghali.

DARREN: Next. What planet are we on?

MARTHA: Zog.

DARREN: Next. What city are we in?

MARTHA: Chicken City.

DARREN: Right...uh... how many questions is that now?

MARTHA: Three.

DARREN: AAH! Right answer!!! AAGGH!

MARTHA yells in shock, her arm jolts upwards, splashing the drink over her.

DARREN: Oh God that wasn't meant to happen.

MARTHA: What the hell are you doing you bloody lunatic?

DARREN: No, no, no, shit, sorry...I was just...

MARTHA: Suddenly yelling like that. Top of your lungs. You're a public menace. Should be locked up.

DARREN: I was fucking with you, that's all. Bit of fun. Yeah?

LOGAN comes over laughing.

LOGAN: That was priceless, absolutely priceless. Good skills Wham.

MARTHA: You know this idiot?

LOGAN: Wham. This is Martha.

DARREN: Martha? *That* Martha?

MARTHA: You're *friends* with this psychopath?

DARREN: I've got better things to do than stay here to be insulted.

MARTHA: Don't then.

LOGAN: Let's have a drink one day man. OK?

DARREN: Fine. Don't bring her.

DARREN exits. LOGAN laughs.

LOGAN: I think you hurt his feelings.

MARTHA: *His* feelings?

LOGAN: Need another? Usual?

She nods, he goes. Lights change. MARTHA addresses the audience.

MARTHA: It was my first day at a new school. I was thirteen. We'd moved for my Dad's work. It was my own fault I was late, I'm easily distracted. I walked into the classroom, all these eyes on me. Mr. Proudlock was furious. "Who are *you*?" "Martha Wiggly" I said. "Why are you late Wiggly?" I froze. Then this skinny boy in the back spoke up. "Her bus broke down sir," he said. Lying. "I passed it on my way in. Noticed her standing on the pavement." "Very well then," said Proudlock, "sit." There was one seat left. Next to his.

Lights change.

LOGAN: *(Returning.)* Vodka, lime, soda and cranberry. Still don't know how you can drink that muck.

MARTHA: Can we talk about something?

LOGAN: Yes. *Can* we?

MARTHA: Uh…yes. I just…

LOGAN: cos I really want to run something by you.

MARTHA: Oh. Great because…

LOGAN: I've been doing some thinking.

MARTHA: Oh.

LOGAN: Yes. About Jenny.

MARTHA: Oh.

LOGAN: About.

MARTHA: Oh.

LOGAN: …You know…

MARTHA: What is it, are things, I mean, ok?

LOGAN: Yes. No. Yes. Great.

MARTHA: Oh.

LOGAN: Well not great exactly.

MARTHA: Oh.

LOGAN: I mean we aren't…just…*sexually*…

MARTHA: *Oooohhh* Logan no no…no I don't think I should really…

LOGAN: That's why I've decided to ask her to move in with me. Take it to the next level.

MARTHA: What? I mean. What? I mean. When did you decide this?

16

LOGAN: There's just something about her... Even her name. Jenny Sanchez. It's pretty amazing don't you think?

MARTHA: *(She doesn't.)* Yes, yes it is, but haven't you just met this woman, I mean, how much do you really know about her?

LOGAN: I know she's an artist.

MARTHA: Well. She designs websites...but yes...ok...I just, you know, cos when I asked you're always...

LOGAN: But there's a point, isn't there, in your life, isn't there, where you want to just...you can't spend your adulthood tricking people into liking you, you have put down roots. Build a life with someone. Right?

MARTHA: God. I don't know what to say. I'm just...really... surprised...

LOGAN: I thought you'd be happy.

MARTHA: *Happy?*

LOGAN: You're always telling me to grow up.

MARTHA: Yes, oh, I am...happy. Yes. I'm delirious.

MARTHA drinks. LOGAN makes a cheers gesture and drinks. MARTHA smiles to cover her crushing disappointment.

A bell rings. Ding ding. Lights change. Music.

GAME THREE – ROLE PLAYING

Lights up on LOGAN sitting on the end of a bed opposite Candy, who wears a funky wig.

LOGAN: What's your name?

CANDY: Candy.

LOGAN: Not very Russian.

CANDY: I am from Belarus.

LOGAN: Right.

Awkward silence. They look at each other coyly.

LOGAN: Minsk.

CANDY: Uh?

LOGAN: The capital of Belarus. Minsk. I'm a keen geographer. So…

CANDY: So you want something off menu or what?

LOGAN: Menu?

CANDY: You not see menu?

LOGAN: I don't think so.

CANDY: Blow job; Twenty five pounds. Toe sucking; fifteen … per toe.

LOGAN: Fifteen quid?

CANDY: Per toe.

LOGAN: That's a tad steep.

CANDY: You want I suck toe?

LOGAN: Not really.

CANDY: Then why you argue for?

LOGAN: Sorry.

CANDY: Sixty niner; sixty nine.

LOGAN: Oh good to see there's a bit of humour injected into the...

CANDY: Straight screw – fifty. Water-sports – thirty five.

LOGAN: That's very reasonable. I mean comparative to the toe sucking.

CANDY: You want I piss in your mouth?

LOGAN: What?

CANDY: You want I piss in your mouth? Water-sports?

LOGAN: Uh, no, I was just talking...

CANDY: I am highly accurate.

LOGAN: I'm not querying your aim...

CANDY: I get you in eye I discount you ten pounds.

LOGAN: Let's park that then shall we?

CANDY: Ok. Cartwheel – seventy five.

LOGAN: What's a cartwheel?

CANDY: Yah. I not think you ready for Cartwheel.

LOGAN: Hang on, I resent that.

CANDY: So? What you choose? Time is money.

LOGAN: Oh yes. Parkinson's Law.

CANDY: What you say?

LOGAN: A job expands to fill the time given to achieve it. Or is that something else?

CANDY: You want to talk? Sixty pound.

LOGAN: What?

CANDY: You want just talk. Sixty pound. You pay now.

LOGAN: Sixty quid? But that's pricier than screwing.

CANDY: Is harder work. You want talking. Sixty pound.

CANDY holds out her hand.

LOGAN: How much was it for a blow job again?

CANDY: You talk too much.

CANDY kneels down and unzips LOGAN's trousers.

LOGAN: Well I'm a teacher, you need to be able to…

CANDY's goes to work on LOGAN's nether regions.

LOGAN: Uhm…communicate.

CANDY: Hello, we do have the signs of life.

LOGAN: My Dad was the opposite. He never spoke. Never. Very…Especially at difficult moments. Emotional moments. A religious man. A Calvinist. Predestination. That's what they believe. Calvinists. They believe, you know, that what…whatever you do in life…good bad, atrocious…totally irrelevant…doesn't matter, cos your destiny's figured out before your birth. It's no wonder he stepped in front of the 139 bus.

CANDY stops, pulls away, and rips off her wig, becoming JENNY.

JENNY: Jesus…

LOGAN: You know the 139? Goes from Oxford Street down West End lane, West Hampstead way...Dennington Park Road...what's wrong?

JENNY: I knew you'd bottle it.

LOGAN: That wig was freaking me out.

JENNY: I knew you wouldn't go through with this...you're so uptight.

LOGAN: Maybe I'm not as intrepid as you, ok...

JENNY: You didn't even try Logan. Yapping on about the 139 bus.

LOGAN: ...it's just a little intimidating when you're giving such a confident rendition of a Belarusian hooker.

JENNY: I was role-playing.

LOGAN: Well who knew you were Judy fucking Dench? I mean all that stuff about menus and toe sucking and fucking cartwheels? Have you done this before?

JENNY: ...*Excuse me*?

LOGAN: I mean you didn't miss a beat, you were so well versed.

JENNY: Oh now I see what this is about. You hate it that I might've been kinky with someone else. That's what turned your cock into a frightened raisin.

LOGAN: So you *have*. You have done this with someone else?

JENNY: Oh God.

LOGAN: How many times? Once? Several? More than several? Is posing as a prostitute something you're particularly skilled at? Can you be hired out for weddings and barmitvahs?

JENNY: That's what terrifies you isn't it? You can't stand the thought I might actually *lust*, might actually *feel* lust. Might actually be driven by *lust*.

LOGAN: Can you stop saying lust?

JENNY: If you knew half the shit that goes through my head your whole world would implode.

Pause.

LOGAN: Well...this evening has certainly been an eye-opener...

JENNY: How did we even get together in the first place?

Pause.

JENNY: I did this because I care about you, you numpty, and I want this to work and it isn't. Not physically.

LOGAN: I mean...

JENNY: ...and if one of us doesn't take charge of this relationship, then it won't make it. It'll shrivel up and die.

LOGAN: That's why I got a key cut.

Pause.

JENNY: You...

LOGAN: I thought...change gear...I thought if we lived together...maybe that would...maybe I'd feel more... comfortable.

JENNY: Right.

LOGAN: So? What do you think?

DARREN enters. He begins to change into a pair of baggy, multi-coloured trousers and a bizarre floppy hat. He addresses the audience.

DARREN: Some of you started judging me a while back. That's cool. We're all trying to figure out where the boundaries are, I get that. And sure, my methods are unorthodox: push and pull, stay one step ahead, throw in a curve-ball when least expected, but, shit, that's the game. Yeah? And while you sit there and judge, just think about this. Think about your own lives. Think about how you all crave affirmation. How we're all selling ourselves all the time. Today, for example, there's a room up for rent in my flat. The Love Shack. Got people coming to see it. So, I'm selling. Not just the room, the whole package. It's on for six hundred, but, watch, I'm gonna get whoever it is so juiced up about living here they'll offer me six fifty. Just to be part of the adventure.

Buzz at door.

DARREN: OK. They're here. Keep focused, I'm gonna be changing gears all over the place.

Buzz at the door. DARREN opens the door to MARTHA.

DARREN: First thing that comes into your head when you see this hat?

MARTHA: Learning difficulties.

DARREN: What?

MARTHA: The agency said five o'clock.

DARREN: *Learning difficulties?*

MARTHA: Sorry, you look amazingly familiar, have we met…?

23

DARREN: Highly possible, I'm a social Exocet, a shape shifter. Come in then, come in. *(He takes off his hat forlornly.)*

MARTHA: Oh I've upset you.

DARREN: No.

MARTHA: Yes. You're upset.

DARREN: Bounces off me. Bounces straight off me. Anyway. Start over. Positivity. Keep moving. Welcome to the dream flat.

MARTHA: Dream flat? Well it is quite roomy I suppose. Near the tube.

DARREN: Ok. That's not why it's the dream flat.

MARTHA: God! Yes. I know where I recognise you from now! You're *Wham*!

DARREN: Oh. Uh…well…

MARTHA: Yes, that's right, I met you with Logan last month.

DARREN: Logan, right.

MARTHA: Tried to chat me up with that obnoxious quiz.

DARREN: I'm out a lot babe…you know…

MARTHA: …the agency said your name was Darren.

DARREN: Darren.

MARTHA: Do you normally tell people you're called Wham?

DARREN: What's normal? Who's normal? Are you?

MARTHA: What? *Me*? I mean…

DARREN: Oh I suppose you're gonna diagnose me. That's what happens now isn't it. Everyone's got a mental disorder.

MARTHA: I really wasn't.

Awkward pause.

DARREN: So how is the old bastard?

MARTHA: Fine. In love. Jenny Sanchez. Do you think that's
an especially amazing name.

DARREN: She sounds hot.

MARTHA: He's moving her in. Lock stock and barrel. Is that
the kitchen through there?

DARREN: Didn't know he had it in him.

MARTHA: Logan? He's got a sort of grumpy thing that's not
completely unattractive, the agency said management fees
were included in the price.

DARREN: OK, fine, if you're gonna play hard ball. Why
is this the Dream Flat? It's the *dream flat* because this is
where the magic happens.

MARTHA: Is it?

DARREN: Live fast, play hard. Parties, chilling, whatever.
Hanging. Or just vibe-ing out, anything goes you know
what I'm saying?

MARTHA: *(She doesn't.)* Yes, yes I do. So six hundred
including fees then?

DARREN: What about the trousers?

MARTHA: What?

DARREN: The trousers.

MARTHA: ...the...?

DARREN: Since you don't like the hat. Little boutique down Soho. Trendy as all hell and defo not cheap, but you get what you pay for.

MARTHA: It's just I can't really go higher than five really. I'm not in a hugely well-paid job, just need a place to sleep, near work.

DARREN: I dig that, what's your skills?

MARTHA: Well, like I say, I'm a...

DARREN: Yeah cos I'm kind of like a city analyst. Yeah. High level shit. Sure, probably seems glamorous to the likes of you...But honestly? It's hard freaking graft man, you feel me? So, yeah, I'm just doing it till I burn myself out. Then on to the next mountain. Probably sounds pretty macho for your tastes, a tad masculine for your palette, but, shit, I don't shirk from that. I'm a leader, I'm a *Caesar*, I can't help that, it's in my DNA. Deep Natural Attitude.

MARTHA: Is this really how you talk? I mean all the time?

DARREN: Shit sorry. Is it too "high level" for you? That's what you get living here; wall to wall banter. You can't stop it, you just can't stop it.

MARTHA: That's why it's the mad flat is it?

DARREN: Dream flat. You're getting a *lifestyle experience.* Live like you mean it. Funky flat, funky, clothes, funky life. Let the world judge. Bring it on.

MARTHA: Yes but surely don't go outside dressed in that jester's costume?

DARREN: Jester's cost...that's a bit rich when you're head to toe in H and M.

MARTHA: What? Oh...well...

DARREN: No, no, it's suits you, that dress. Really. Thrifty.

MARTHA: It was a gift actually, from my aunt.

DARREN: Hey look, I don't judge, I'm sure she's got plenty of other qualities. Just, taste isn't one of them.

MARTHA: Well no because she's dead.

DARREN: Oh. God. I…

MARTHA: We were really close, actually, she practically brought me up.

DARREN: Right. Shit…look…I'm really sorry.

MARTHA: Really horrible skin condition. She just flaked away.

DARREN: F…what? Flaked away?

MARTHA: Flaked completely away. Bills included is it?

DARREN: Sorry?

MARTHA: Gas, electricity…?

DARREN: Separate. Listen that's a horrible story. About your aunt. Flaking away like that.

MARTHA: I'm just fucking with you. She's not dead. So my room would be this one at the end is that right?

DARREN: What?

MARTHA: *(Crosses the stage to look in at the room.)* Smaller than I expected.

DARREN: *(Follows.)* Uh. Yeah. Sorry, sorry…*sorry*…you were joking?

MARTHA: Yeah.

DARREN: That's pretty dark you know?

27

MARTHA: What's the matter, can't you take it? Bit of banter.

DARREN: I...

MARTHA: Didn't mean to be too "*high level*".

DARREN: Now listen here...listen here...whatever your name is.

MARTHA: You know I think I'll take the room.

DARREN: What? Really?

MARTHA: If you're friends with Logan you can't be all bad.

DARREN: Knew it. Knew you'd take it. Soon as you walked in here.

MARTHA: Convenient for work. But, really, I can't go higher than four-fifty.

DARREN: It was on at six...

MARTHA: At least you know I won't run off without paying. Deal?

MARTHA puts out her hand. DARREN stands slack jawed for a moment.

DARREN: Fine. Four-fifty. For a friend of Logan's.

They shake hands. MARTHA smiles a triumphant smile then walks around the room breathing it in.

MARTHA: Yes. I think I might like it here.

LOGAN's house. JENNY is unpacking boxes. LOGAN brings in a box.

LOGAN: One more big one and a lamp.

JENNY: And my laptop. It's in the front seat.

LOGAN: Got it.

JENNY: Cheers.

> *LOGAN puts the box down and goes. JENNY waits for him to go, then checks her phone.*

JENNY: What the hootenanny?

> *A text alert sounds from LOGAN's phone, which is on a shelf. JENNY, checking LOGAN is not around, picks up his phone and looks at it. She frowns.*
>
> *Hearing LOGAN returning, JENNY quickly replaces the phone. LOGAN reappears with a big cardboard box, a standard lamp and a laptop resting on the box.*

LOGAN: Little help! Sanchez!

JENNY: Careful! There's wine in that one. Decent bottles.

> *LOGAN slams down the box.*

LOGAN: I told you to label them.

JENNY: And that laptop's got my whole life on it. What're you trying to prove, you nutter? *(She checks the bottles.)*

LOGAN: They ok?

JENNY: Fine. Shall I open one? Celebrate?

LOGAN: Capital idea, I'll start unpacking the boxes.

JENNY: *(As she goes.)* K.

Alone, LOGAN uses his phone to put some music on the sound system, then starts unpacking one of the boxes. He pulls out some books. He pulls out a weird looking doll, with one eye hanging out of its socket. He holds up the doll and grimaces.

LOGAN: What the hootenanny?

JENNY returns with two glasses of wine.

LOGAN: Uhm…what the fuck is this?

JENNY: What? Oh… *(Shit.)*…

LOGAN: It's a tad alarming.

JENNY: Oh you mean Nancy?

LOGAN: Nancy?

JENNY: She was my aunt's. Here.

JENNY hands LOGAN a glass.

LOGAN: She looks like been through some serious shit. What've you been doing to her?

JENNY: She's old. Cheers then. *(Raises her glass.)* Housemates.

LOGAN: *(Clinking his glass with hers.)* Why's she got an eye hanging out?

JENNY: *(Drinking.)* Mmm. Told you this wine was the shit.

LOGAN: You don't have it on the bed do you? That's gonna put me off my game.

JENNY looks around at the space.

JENNY: I could transform this place, you know, hardly take any effort. You don't mind if stick a few prints up, do you?

LOGAN: …it's not from your ex then?

JENNY: Excuse me?

LOGAN: The doll. Didn't you once tell me your ex bought you one present in the whole four years you went out with him?

JENNY: Right.

LOGAN: Went down the charity shop and bought you some crappy doll. For your birthday.

JENNY: I told you that?

LOGAN: Yes.

Pause. They stare at each other.

JENNY: Ok look. *(Downs her wine.)* Let's crack on shall we, I need to…

LOGAN: …what's the hurry…

JENNY: Oh, I…

LOGAN: I thought we'd get a take-away, christen the bed…

JENNY: …God I'd love to, honestly, that sounds…just fucking perfect…

LOGAN: Jenny…

JENNY: … but I promised I'd got to this dinner tonight…

LOGAN: *Tonight?*

JENNY: Work thing, I did tell you…

LOGAN: You definitely didn't.

JENNY: You don't mind, do you?

LOGAN: No, no, I…it's…

JENNY: It's really important, this big new client, I'll be right back, then we can…

LOGAN: …totally fine…

JENNY: …snuggle.

LOGAN: Great.

JENNY: I'll get ready then. Wish me luck.

LOGAN: Good luck.

JENNY goes. LOGAN turns off the music.

MARTHA is moving her stuff into the flat. DARREN helps with boxes.

DARREN: So you're a radiographer? That's, like, x-rays and shit yeah?

MARTHA: My dad tells people I look at bones for a living.

DARREN: You see through people's skin. Can't get more naked than that.

MARTHA: Don't try to make it sound erotic. It's not erotic.

DARREN: *(Trying to sound erotic.)* Maybe you could put me under your x-ray. Check out my bones.

MARTHA: See what I mean? *(About a box.)* Could you put that down here?

DARREN: Sure thing. *(Puts down a box and pulls a small, lumpy looking Buddha from a box.)* What the hell is *this*?

MARTHA: I saw him next to a fish tank in a Chinese restaurant. He looked so remarkably like my x-boyfriend, I had to have him.

DARREN: Bit on the tubby side was he, your ex?

MARTHA: I don't go for good-looking people.

DARREN: Why? Do we intimidate you?

MARTHA: *(Retrieving the Buddha.)* There was this one lad. Tom. Beautiful man, really took your breath away.

DARREN: Toms tend to be good looking.

MARTHA: It was quite intimidating. Women always staring, the constant gaze, all these hot eyes, I felt so anxious I had to end it. In a Costa's of all places. *(Deciding where to place the Buddha.)* Is this a good place for it?

33

DARREN: Perfection.

MARTHA: *(Goes to another box.)* I regretted it the moment he walked away. Felt so stupid. I tried to get up and go after him, but I'd just bought these new jeans and they were really tight and I tripped and fell flat on my face.

DARREN: Classic.

MARTHA: I texted him later to say I'd made a mistake but he'd met someone one the bus. Can you believe it?

DARREN: Sure. Toms.

MARTHA: Tell me about it.

She smiles.

DARREN: There's that smile.

DARREN leans in, gazing into MARTHA's eyes. There is an intensely intimate moment between them, finally broken when MARTHA moves away.

MARTHA: I'd better get back to…

DARREN: Yeah. Yes.

MARTHA gets back to unpacking.

DARREN: But seriously, though, I'm, really, so glad it's you moving in and not some…you know…leggy, scorching hot…you know.

MARTHA: Oh. Well…

DARREN: I mean it's really such a relief, you know, because there's absolutely no chance of us…*ever*…you know… having…

MARTHA: Look.

DARREN: Sex. What?

MARTHA: I mean why would you even…?

DARREN: No, no, I'm not… I mean you're not a monster I'm not saying that.

MARTHA: Oh. Good then…

DARREN: So it's handy. Is what I'm saying. There won't be any, you know, *awkward moments.*

MARTHA: You mean apart from this one?

DARREN: See I know myself. If I lived with an eight or nine, you know it'd get messy. But with a six and a half…

MARTHA: *Six and a half!*

DARREN: No, you're spot on. Where do want this lamp?

MARTHA: I can manage, thank you.

MARTHA grabs the lamp, in a fury, plonks it down, angrily shifting it into place.

DARREN: *(Watches her.)* Hey I…I didn't offend you did I?

MARTHA: Certainly not. Certainly not.

DARREN: I mean I was just saying…

MARTHA: No it's all good, it's all good, it's all…because I'm actually, as it happens, seeing someone. So.

DARREN: Seeing someone?

MARTHA: A doctor. As it happens. If you must ask. Yes.

DARREN: I didn't know you were…

MARTHA: Yes he is. Actually. He's pretty bloody wonderful. Fabulous bedside…bedside manner. Actually. So nothing…*between you and me*…Could *ever…ever* happen. I could never betray Doctor Roberts.

DARREN: Right. Hang on…

MARTHA: Really, I couldn't live with myself. I'm completely devoted to him.

DARREN: *Doctor Roberts*?

MARTHA: Sorry?

DARREN: You called him *Doctor* Roberts?

MARTHA: Did I?

DARREN: Yes.

MARTHA: Well that's his name. Doctor David Roberts.

DARREN: Bit odd isn't it?

MARTHA: What's odd?

DARREN: Referring to your boyfriend as *Doctor* Roberts.

MARTHA: Well I mean he's not…you know…he's not *exactly*…I mean we're not, you know, like…*official* or anything.

DARREN: Right. So…what… you're seeing him?

MARTHA: Well yes… I do …I do *see* him.

DARREN: You…?

MARTHA: I mean we work in the same department so I definitely, you know I definitely *(Coughs.)* see him.

DARREN: Oh my God…

MARTHA: I mean I'm forever watching him. Some days I can't take my eyes of him.

DARREN: You're stalking him?!

MARTHA: NO!

DARREN: Have you actually had any kind of contact with this man?

MARTHA: Of course I've had contact with him.

DARREN: I mean *outside* of a work situation.

MARTHA: In my head we've had all kinds of contact.

DARREN: In your head?

MARTHA: ...and not just contact, but complex, glorious conversations. We cover great topics, vast philosophical terrains, we put the world to rights.

DARREN: Oh my God...

MARTHA: Maybe it's better this way. I can't screw it up. I can't say something gigantically stupid and foul it all up.

DARREN: Oh man. This is really tragic...I mean it breaks my heart to hear this, it really does, you've no idea...

MARTHA: Leave me alone. I've got unpacking to do. You're distracting me.

DARREN: I could teach you some techniques. They could transform your whole perspective.

MARTHA: Are you joking?

DARREN: I'm a bedroom warrior.

MARTHA: No. No Darren. You're a sad, desperate nerd who thinks he can impress women by acting like a massive poser.

DARREN: These techniques have been honed. Ok? Extensively tested in-field. With great success.

MARTHA: You tried it on me remember? I thought you were the most colossal dickhead. I thought you were a joke.

DARREN: *I'm* a joke? *I'm* a joke? "Oh I *see* Dr Roberts. With my long lens binoculars."

MARTHA: Right. Yes. I deserve that. I'm sorry I said you were a desperate nerd.

DARREN: Totally fine.

He starts to leave.

MARTHA: Where're you going?

DARREN: There're more boxes in the car.

MARTHA: But I was so rude to you.

DARREN: Forget it. Happy to do it.

Beat. MARTHA nods. DARREN exits.

GAME SEVEN – SHADOW BOXING

LOGAN and JENNY's house. LOGAN is there. The shower is running.

JENNY enters. She is in a dressing gown, drying her hair with a towel.

JENNY: Oh. Hey. Good swim?

LOGAN: Yeah. Jenny…

JENNY: I was gonna heat up some of that stew.

LOGAN: Who was the dude?

JENNY: The *dude?*

LOGAN: That was here before.

JENNY: I don't understand.

LOGAN: Don't you?

JENNY: Why are you looking at me like that?

LOGAN: I didn't go swimming.

JENNY: What?

LOGAN: I forgot my trunks, so I came home…saw someone leaving my house.

JENNY: Leaving *your* house?

LOGAN: Yes.

JENNY: Leaving *our* house.

LOGAN: I've been sitting outside in the car for ten minutes. Just…

JENNY: His name's Felix. He's a client. I was doing some work for him and he came over to discuss it. Ok?

LOGAN: Do you usually see clients at home?

39

JENNY: He was in the neighbourhood. He had some thoughts.

LOGAN: Oh he had some thoughts did he?

JENNY: Sorry, I didn't know I had to run all my work meetings by you...

LOGAN: ...he couldn't email over his *thoughts*?

JENNY: Is this why you had that key cut? So you could keep tabs on me?

LOGAN: Look...

JENNY: So you can *control* me? Is that it?! Make sure I conduct myself in the correct manner, like a good little girl! Is that why?

LOGAN: Why were you in the shower?

JENNY: What?

LOGAN: You just took a shower.

JENNY: You want me to walk around dirty?

LOGAN: What?

JENNY: I didn't have a shower with him in the house, I waited till he left.

LOGAN: I mean it's...odd...isn't it? You hurl yourself under the shower the moment he's gone.

JENNY: ...ok...

LOGAN: ...lathering up the instant he's gone...no decent interval...

JENNY: This is not acceptable, ok, I will not be bullied by you...

LOGAN: Sorry. Yeah. I think I'm gonna need to hear you say it.

JENNY: …say what?

LOGAN: I need to hear you say you're not fucking him.

Pause. JENNY glares at LOGAN, a long hard death stare.

JENNY: Why does Martha sign off her texts to you with three kisses?

LOGAN: *What?!*

JENNY: I mean does that seem normal to you?

LOGAN: Hang on…

JENNY: Don't you think it's a tad excessive?

LOGAN: You went through my phone?!

JENNY: You told me there was nothing between you two.

LOGAN: You read my messages Jenny? You went through my phone?

JENNY: Do you sign off with three kisses to her?

LOGAN: …how would it look otherwise…

JENNY: You never sent me three kisses.

LOGAN: Because I give you three dimensional kisses, d'you really need virtual ones as well?

JENNY: You and her…always…sharing things…

LOGAN: Jenny…

JENNY: … finishing each other's sentences, ordering each other's meals, playing your little games, joking about people I don't know…

LOGAN: We've known each other forever, what do you want me to do Jenny, just ditch her?

JENNY: I want to know what's between you and that kiss happy cunt!

Pause. Bell rings.

GAME EIGHT – THREE WORD SENTENCES

MARTHA enters in a state.

MARTHA: Stupid, stupid, stupid. God. God. God.

> *She hears DARREN coming in and composes herself. DARREN crashes in. He has a bizarre outfit on, very gaudy and attention seeking.*

DARREN: Crown me the grandmaster of seduction.

MARTHA: *(Pulls herself together and wipes her eyes.)* Oh God.

DARREN: I am the King, the Emperor and the Generalissimo all rolled into one massive charm-machine. I have seen and conquered and come. You want to know details don't you? Of course you do, it's only natural. Saw this eight and half out of ten sitting in the window at Rotisserie Chicken…

MARTHA: That's really great Darren, but I just need a little bit of quiet. Sorry.

DARREN: Oh. Yeah sure. You ok?

MARTHA: Just a bit of a headache.

DARREN: Tough day at the bone factory?

MARTHA: Very.

DARREN: You're not staying in again are you?

MARTHA: I want to finish my book.

DARREN: But it's Saturday night.

MARTHA: Is that why you're dressed like an alien?

DARREN: Stand out from the crowd. It's called peacocking. Get a target to notice you it's half the battle.

MARTHA: Well. Enjoy.

DARREN: Come along if you like.

MARTHA: Maybe another time, yeah? You go… and… play peacocks.

DARREN: I worry about you Martha.

MARTHA: Please don't.

DARREN: Something's not right with you. You've been lolloping about.

MARTHA: Really I'm fine. I'm great.

DARREN: I'm not going anywhere until I know you're ok.

MARTHA: Do you want a signed confession? I'm ok. You don't have to water-board it out of me. I'm brilliant. Now go.

DARREN: Let's play a game.

MARTHA: Oh God Darren.

DARREN: One rule. You can only speak in three-word sentences.

MARTHA: To what end?

DARREN: Gives the conversation a framework. Sets boundaries. If you have to think about how you're structuring your answer, you think more about what you're saying.

MARTHA: Ok if I play your game will you go out and leave me in peace?

DARREN: Absolutely. Ready? Three words only, no more no less. I'll start. How are you?

MARTHA: I am fine?

DARREN: Are you really?

MARTHA: Yes I'm fine.

DARREN: Really and truly.

MARTHA: Are you gonna keep asking the same thing?

DARREN: Three word sentences.

MARTHA: Darren…

DARREN: You've been crying.

Pause.

DARREN: What's the matter?

MARTHA: None…o'your business.

DARREN: Play the game.

MARTHA: Up your arse.

DARREN: How's Doctor David?

MARTHA: He's fucking tremendous!

DARREN: So something happened?

MARTHA: *(Sighs.)* Brought him soup.

DARREN: Nice gesture, and?

MARTHA: I slipped over.

DARREN: And spilled it?

MARTHA: All over him.

DARREN: Classic Martha Wiggly.

MARTHA: Three degree burns.

DARREN: That's an exaggeration.

MARTHA: Needed medical treatment.

DARREN: Opportunity for closeness?

MARTHA: With Nurse Forbes.

DARREN: Who's Nurse Forbes?

MARTHA: Big, nasty, skank.

DARREN: She was there?

MARTHA: Slithering over him.

DARREN: That's not good.

MARTHA: No shit Sherlock.

DARREN: Did you apologise?

MARTHA: I ran away.

DARREN: You ran away?

MARTHA: I didn't want to…oh bloody hell this is too hard.

DARREN: Stay with it.

MARTHA: I can't.

DARREN: Stay with it.

MARTHA: It's a disaster.

DARREN: Disasters are good.

MARTHA: In what way?

DARREN: A fun icebreaker.

MARTHA: Disasters are disastrous.

DARREN: Joke with him.

MARTHA: "Enjoy being flayed."

DARREN: Not like that.

MARTHA: I frighten him.

DARREN: Let me help.

MARTHA: Thank you, no.

DARREN: Teach you techniques.

MARTHA: I'd look silly.

DARREN: Works for me.

MARTHA: *You* look silly.

DARREN: Fine, stay miserable.

MARTHA: Thanks, I will.

DARREN: Pathetic martyr complex.

MARTHA: Aggravating, intrusive tosser.

DARREN: Live life Martha.

MARTHA: Game over, Darren.

She goes. Music. Disco Lights. DARREN dances.

GAME NINE – BULLSHIT

Pub. MARTHA brings drinks. LOGAN is shuffling cards.

LOGAN: Remember how to play?

MARTHA: Gins. Yours is a double.

LOGAN: *(Dealing out the cards quickly.)* Aces high. You place down a card or a set and declare: four eights, two kings, three queens.

MARTHA: *(Sips the wrong drink.)* Urrh. This is yours. *(Swaps drinks.)*

LOGAN: The object's to get rid of all your cards, so you try to sneak in more cards than you declare.

MARTHA: Yes.

LOGAN: If your opponent thinks you're bluffing they call "bullshit".

MARTHA: *Bullshit!* I remember.

LOGAN: If you're caught out, you pick up all the cards in the middle. If you're honest, *they* pick them up. Winner's the first one with no cards. It's all about reading the other person. Watching what's going on behind the eyes. Yeah? Listening to the inflection of their words. You start.

They file through their cards.

MARTHA: *(Placing down three cards.)* Three Aces.

LOGAN: *(Placing a card.)* One Ace.

MARTHA: So how're things with the impossibly named Jenny Sanchez? *(Places three cards.)* Two kings.

LOGAN stares into MARTHA's eyes. Smiles. She smiles.

LOGAN: *(Smiles.)* Bullshit.

MARTHA: Bloody hell. *(Takes her cards.)*

LOGAN: So transparent. *(Places a single card.)* Two Kings.

> *MARTHA squints at him, desperately trying to read him. He glares at her. She places down four cards.*

MARTHA: Four aces. Didn't answer my question.

LOGAN: *(Smiles. Beat. Places one card.)* One Queen.

MARTHA: *(Places two cards.)* Two Kings.

LOGAN: The impossibly named Jenny Sanchez is *great.* Really...great. Thank you for asking. *(Placing three cards.)* Three Jacks.

> *MARTHA squints at him. LOGAN glares. She places four cards.*

MARTHA: Three Queens.

> *Pause. He stares at her. She smiles. Holds her breath.*

LOGAN: How's Wham? And his positive vibes? *(Places a card.)* One Jack.

MARTHA: Fine. *(Places three cards.)* Three Jacks. Great. Actually.

LOGAN: Great? *(Places four cards.)* Three tens.

MARTHA: Really...Great. Brilliant. *(Places two cards.)* One ten.

LOGAN: Thought you'd be climbing the walls by now. *(Places three cards.)* Three nines.

MARTHA: No. No. I'm rather enjoying it.

LOGAN: What in the Dream House?

MARTHA: Dream *Flat. (Places two cards.)* One nine.

LOGAN: Bullshit!

MARTHA: Shit.

LOGAN: I can read you like a kindle Martha Wiggly.

MARTHA: Bollocks, bollocks, cock. *(She sweeps up all the cards.)*

LOGAN: You're *rather* enjoying it. *(Places two cards.)* Two eights.

MARTHA: Well, you know… *(Places four cards.)* …he's very… Four Aces…perky.

LOGAN: What about all those…you know… *(Places one card.)* One seven. Cheesy routines?

MARTHA: Least he knows how to grab someone's attention. Sometimes I wonder if that's half the battle. Getting them to notice you. *(Places four cards.)* Four Kings. I think that's admirable.

LOGAN: Admirable?

MARTHA: He even offered to teach me some of his techniques.

LOGAN: Ha. Now *that* is hilarious.

MARTHA: Why is that so hysterical?

LOGAN: *(Places three cards.)* One six.

MARTHA: I'm sorry, I didn't know my love life was so laughably barren.

LOGAN: So what, you're gonna go peacocking?

MARTHA: Maybe… *(Places three cards.)* Three Queens.

LOGAN: Play idiot pranks on men in bars?

MARTHA: Take your turn.

LOGAN: I just can't bear the thought of you embarrassing yourself like that.

MARTHA: Who says I'd embarrass myself?

LOGAN: You told me you thought he was a joke.

MARTHA: Take your turn Logan.

LOGAN: *(Places four cards.)* Four twos.

MARTHA: Bullshit!

LOGAN turns over the cards.

MARTHA: What? Bollocks. *(Martha sweeps up all the cards, her hands now struggling to hold all of them.)* Bollocks, bollocks, cock.

LOGAN: Look…I'm sorry…I didn't know you were so…I dunno…

MARTHA: What? Didn't think I was so what?

LOGAN: Desperate. *(Beat.)* Shit look…what I mean is…

MARTHA: I see. I see. I see.

LOGAN: Look…

MARTHA: That's how you see me. It's so clear now.

LOGAN: I thought you were focussed on your career. I tried to set you up with guys from my school…you always…

MARTHA: Oh Jesus…

LOGAN: Poo poo-ed the idea. Wouldn't even meet them. Like you were kind of…

MARTHA: Yes?

LOGAN: Forget it.

MARTHA: Like I was kind of what?

LOGAN: Take your turn.

MARTHA: Come on, you're the one who can read my every thought.

LOGAN: I obviously upset you.

MARTHA: Asexual? Is that it?

LOGAN: I didn't say that.

MARTHA: You think I don't *feel things*? That I don't have *urges*. You think I'm a block of concrete?

LOGAN: Christ. Take your turn.

MARTHA: I hate this game.

LOGAN: Don't try to weasel out of it cos you're losing, I know you Martha.

MARTHA: No. No, you don't. For someone with such x-ray fucking insight there are things about me that, to you, seem totally invisible.

MARTHA goes. Bell rings.

GAME TEN – CYRANO–ING

Flat. MARTHA and DARREN

MARTHA: Ok let's do it.

DARREN: Great. Do what?

MARTHA: What you said. I've made up my mind.

DARREN: Right. Sorry I really need a steer on this.

MARTHA: Train me up. Teach me how to pull.

DARREN: Oh.

MARTHA: Teach me your powers.

DARREN: Thought you said it was all a joke.

MARTHA: Screw it, what have I got to lose?

DARREN: How much did you drink tonight?

MARTHA: I'm sick of this, sick of waiting, sick of analysing and questioning. I'm shrinking, I'm …I've wasted so much time, I've been standing still for so long, my heart just…I want to act. I want to take life by the balls.

DARREN: Ok, but this is potent stuff yeah? It's not to be taking lightly. This power, in the wrong hands…

MARTHA: Oh come on…you're not handing over nuclear secrets.

DARREN: If we're gonna do this you have to take it seriously. If I pass on my gifts you have to treat them with reverence and respect.

MARTHA: Don't give me that Spiderman bullshit, just tell me how I can get David to go out with me.

DARREN regards MARTHA pensively for a beat.

DARREN: All right. But once I do this, there's no going back. You'll never see social interactions in the same way again. Every exchange, every look, every passing moment of human interplay, even the smallest, most insignificant thing…you'll see it all in a new light. You'll never be the same.

MARTHA: Excellent. Do it. Teach me.

DARREN: OK. First. Understand this. Everything you've ever thought about relationships is bullshit.

MARTHA: Everything?

DARREN: Ok, you see a guy in a bar, a guy you like. Imagine it.

MARTHA: OK. I'm imagining.

DARREN: You start talking, you want him to ask you out, how do you act?

MARTHA: I dunno. Friendly?

DARREN: AH AHHHH! Wrong. Friendly? Where's the challenge in that?

MARTHA: Maybe he doesn't want a challenge?

DARREN: Act friendly, that's exactly what you'll be. Friends. Make him *work* for it. Ok first thing is this. You want him to *notice* you. When you walk into a room, you gotta own that space. Straight back, chest out, head up…proud. Supreme Confidence. Stand out from the crowd. A guy like David, any guy, they don't want a wallflower they want dynamism. When you walk on to that hospital ward tomorrow you want David to turn his head don't you?

MARTHA: I…uh…

DARREN: Do you want him to notice you or not?

MARTHA: Yes.

DARREN: Right. So let's see it. Walk into the room. Rehearse for success.

MARTHA: You want me to show you? Now?

DARREN: How d'you think Lionel Messi scores so many goals? He does it over and over, gets it into his bones. So come on, go out and come back in. And remember; chest out, shoulders back, head up…relaxed, poised…smile, very important to smile…and say to yourself; "I own this whole fucking place."

MARTHA goes out and re-enters stalking in a manic fashion, bobbing up and down, head craned back, chest jutting forward, and a strange grin on her face.

MARTHA: I fucking own this fucking place!

DARREN: Wait, stop. Stop. What the hell was that?

MARTHA: I was owning the room.

DARREN: First. Don't actually say it out loud. You're supposed to be projecting the thought with your body.

MARTHA: Oh. Wasn't I doing that?

DARREN: No. Second. Why were you grinning like that? It's weird.

MARTHA: You said smiling was important.

DARREN: Ok. Look, just relax and try again. It's probably first-time nerves. No-one can be that bad at this. Come in again. Projecting confidence and fun.

MARTHA goes out and re-enters, toning down the walk, but still looking odd.

DARREN: Jesus. OK, we'll work on the walk later. Moving on. You spot the target in the corner of the room and you catch his eye.

MARTHA: The target?

DARREN: Yes. This is a take-down. This David character, he's your prey. Your quarry. To be hunted down. To be dazzled into submission with ruthless precision. Now… a well-placed glance across the room, then a quick look away, will send a signal…a sort of green light. He'll be prompted to come over. Makes him think he's doing the running, when you're the one who initiated it.

MARTHA: That's actually not bad.

DARREN: OK. Let's see the look.

MARTHA looks over and winks.

DARREN: For God's sake.

MARTHA: What?

DARREN: Don't wink. What are you doing?

MARTHA: I'm giving him the green light.

DARREN: Be subtle. Hold a look for a fraction longer than normal and then…very delicately and suggestively…touch the nape of your neck.

MARTHA: Touch my neck?

DARREN: The nape of your neck, yes, very important part of the mating dance, any guy is powerless to resist the touching the neck thing.

MARTHA prods her neck fiercely.

DARREN: Don't jab at it like that, what are you doing?

MARTHA: Sorry.

DARREN: It's supposed to be delicate, suggestive… Christ. Right, I want you to practice that in your own time. The neck thing is big. OK. Pressing on. The approach. When you go over to him, don't convey too much interest. Be aloof.

MARTHA: I'm not sure I can do aloof.

DARREN: It's easy, just…you step into his eyeline, but don't look at him.

MARTHA: How the hell do I do that?

DARREN: I dunno, go up to his friend. Who does he hang out with? Another doctor, a nurse? We need a patsy.

MARTHA: Oh. He often chats to Kenny the lab technician.

DARREN: Kenny sounds perfect. So. Go up to Kenny, ignoring the target.

MARTHA: Ignore him?

DARREN: Look, this guy is a handsome doctor, he's got his pick of women at that hospital. I bet they all fawn over him don't they, giggle at his lame jokes …

MARTHA: That's absolutely what they do.

DARREN: Right. So you gotta change the rules on him. Bend the system to your advantage. How do you do that? By *isolating* the target. By making him feel like he's out in the cold looking in, desperate to be part of your fun world.

MARTHA: Oh.

DARREN: Say you start talking to Kenny about some, I dunno, juicy piece of office gossip, completely ignoring, by the way, Doctor David. Suddenly the power passes to you. Now it's in your gift to allow him into the conversation. He won't be used to that, it'll confuse him, it's how you lure him into your trap.

MARTHA: That actually pretty good. Ok so I go up to Kenny.

DARREN: And say something playful…like…I dunno talk about lube.

MARTHA: What?

DARREN: Say something provocative.

MARTHA: Lube?

DARREN: Come on. Show me the approach. I'll be Kenny.

MARTHA: *(Lopes over, clearly ignoring the imaginary David.)* Hey Kenny I found all this lube. What shall I do with it?

DARREN: Oh God, what's that?

MARTHA: What? I…

DARREN: You're meant to be having a laugh with the dude, not stock taking.

MARTHA: Well I never started a conversation about lube before.

DARREN: Just say, I dunno something like; "Have you heard about Jan and Steve from accounts? They were caught in the store cupboard covered in cling film and lube…word is they were sloshing about like eels in a bucket."

MARTHA: I'm not saying that.

DARREN: You're just trying to grab the target's attention. Say something he feels duty bound to remark upon then slam him down.

MARTHA: How do I do that? I never slammed anyone down.

DARREN: It's easy. When he tries to speak you say something like; "This one's keen." And give him like a teasing nick name. Like… "Pipe down Doctor Boner. Didn't your Mum tell you it's rude to interrupt?"

MARTHA: Doctor Boner? What's that supposed to be?

DARREN: Cos of the x-rays.

MARTHA: But he's in general surgery, not orthopaedics…

DARREN: Doesn't matter, it's a hook. A fun…look. Just. Try it. Come on.

MARTHA: "Pipe down Doctor Boner! Don't interrupt. Didn't your Mummy bring you up properly?"

DARREN: Yeah or say. "You've got a very pushy personality. Were you beaten as a child?" Pick out his flaws. Make him feel vulnerable. Break him down so only you can raise him back up. Then…see… when *you* compliment him it'll actually *mean* something. Seduction is all push and pull, it's all about controlling how people feel towards you. Making him crave your approval.

MARTHA: I don't think I'm gonna be very good at this. It's late. Maybe I should sleep on it. See how I feel tomorrow…

DARREN: Tomorrow is bullshit! The only thing that's real is now. This moment. When you go into that hospital tomorrow the only person this David will be interested in speaking to is you. Because you're fucking great. You're witty and warm and complicated and anyone who goes out with you is a lucky bastard. You can do this Martha I know you can, I believe in you. Now show me that walk again. Then I'll teach you the kiss-close.

INTERVAL

Entr'acte

DARREN: For several millennia after we climbed out of the primordial soup, we had a fail-safe method of courtship. A man'd find a woman he liked, crack her over the head and drag her to his cave.

MARTHA: ...we had clans, tribes, religions...developed rules; structures,

LOGAN: ...financial arrangements, betrothals. dowries, land, property...

DARREN: Love became commercialised. Monetised. Globalised.

LOGAN: Once tribal affiliations decided whom you loved, now it was, what?

MARTHA: Now to build a meaningful relationship we relied on...what?

DARREN: A shared taste in Mexican food and a passion for Will Ferrell movies.

LOGAN: We relied on timing, luck, geography...

DARREN: Booze?

JENNY: Generous lighting.

MARTHA: A sense of spatial awareness is also useful. Just as a tip.

DARREN: Now we had to rely on our own charm, our own discretion...

LOGAN: Our own foresight and our own judgement.

JENNY: And that's when the wheels came off the wagon.

MARTHA: But what is this urge? This inner fire? What is the meaning of it?

LOGAN: A biological trick? Nature duping us with hormones and endorphins...

JENNY: ...an animal urge, chemicals in the body: combining and colluding, responding to a what...

DARREN: Reacting to...what...a signal, a trigger.

MARTHA: A smell, a smile, a curve of the...

JENNY: Love urges us on. Urges us to connect, to reproduce...

DARREN: Because of this deep seated...

LOGAN: The need, yes, the deep, deep need...

DARREN: We had an obligation, a primal obligation to...

JENNY: ...this profound need to continue the species...

LOGAN: An expression of the holiest of holies...the purest manifestation of God, or of the order of the entire cosmos...

DARREN: Then we developed algorithms...

LOGAN: Everyone connecting to everyone else. Everyone disclosing their deepest...

JENNY: Now you could know more about some complete stranger than you did about your own friends. Your own family.

DARREN: ...the apps, the swiping, the ghosting, the cat fishing, the orbiting.

MARTHA: We...became players in a massive virtual game of...

JENNY: …became avatars, became digital chess pieces being moved around a board.

LOGAN: We became atomised, digitised, disconnected from the physical…

DARREN: But there, underneath…some prehistoric instinct remains, simmering away…

MARTHA: But haven't we all been part of an experiment? Part of this human laboratory…

JENNY: And doesn't a river run through us all, of desire. An inner fire that is an affirmation.

DARREN: Yes. An affirmation of life.

MARTHA: Is an affirmation of the urge to make life and to justify it. Is the very point and meaning of life itself.

Act Two

GAME ELEVEN – GREEN-EYED MONSTER

Pub: LOGAN and DARREN get drinks and sit at a table.

LOGAN: … So. You and Martha. Living together. *Weird.*

DARREN: Yeah.

They drink.

LOGAN: So how's it going?

DARREN: Great.

LOGAN: *Great?* Really?

DARREN: Well…you know…good. Fine.

LOGAN: You *said* great.

DARREN: Well…you know…she's…

LOGAN: Yes?

DARREN: You know…she's…

LOGAN: She's what?

DARREN: You know…clean.

LOGAN: Clean?

DARREN: Yes. Clean.

LOGAN: She's *clean?*

DARREN: Well…you know…she you know… keeps her head down, pays her bills, she's, you know… perfect housemate.

LOGAN: So she's *perfect?*

DARREN: Can we talk about something else?

LOGAN: Sure.

Awkward pause.

LOGAN: So there's nothing that bothers you...

DARREN: Christ...

LOGAN: Nothing that niggles at you at all...

DARREN: ...I mean I suppose she does...you know...mope about a bit...

LOGAN: Mopes about?

DARREN: ... pining after, yes, some doctor bloke.

LOGAN: What bloke?

DARREN: Oh my God...have you met him? David.

LOGAN: Never, but I definitely want to smack him.

DARREN: I've never met him, but I can tell he's got one of those faces.

LOGAN: You want to punch?

DARREN: I detest him.

LOGAN: Well you've always been an excellent judge of character mate.

DARREN: So have you mate, put yourself on that list. An immaculate judge.

LOGAN: Well thank you, I appreciate that.

DARREN: And you can't say we don't give people a fair crack at the whip.

LOGAN: I'd like to see 'em try it.

LOGAN nods, thoughtfully. They drink.

LOGAN: So what else annoys you about her?

DARREN: What?

LOGAN: Other than her moping about after this David cocksucker...

DARREN: ...look, I never said it...

LOGAN: What else irks you about living with her?

DARREN: Nothing.

LOGAN: Nothing at all, there's nothing that aggravates you about her at all?

DARREN: ...well...

LOGAN: I'm listening.

DARREN: I suppose she can be a tad condescending.

LOGAN: Superior. Looks down her nose at you, is it?

DARREN: I could do with her turning the volume down on the snootiness. Yes. Ok. But like I say, like I said before, other than that...

LOGAN: Other than the fact she mopes about and makes you feel small...other than that...?

DARREN: ...other than that...

LOGAN: Other than that, she's perfect.

DARREN: Yes.

LOGAN glares at DARREN. DARREN shifts awkwardly. They drink.

LOGAN: Right. Well. I'm really happy for you, mate. Really.

LOGAN drinks deeply, DARREN watches LOGAN, something dawning on him.

DARREN: Look, if you're uncomfortable with this…if you got a problem with us…living together…

LOGAN: No, no, it's…

DARREN: Cos there's a code. Right? Between men. Between guys like us. And if this whole, you know…*scenario*…if it's making you…

LOGAN: Why? What would you do?

DARREN: I…what?

LOGAN: If I had a problem. What would you do?

DARREN: So you *are* uncomfortable?

LOGAN: Let's say I was. Would you boot her out?

DARREN: Boot her out?!

LOGAN: Cos that's really, I mean that's the least I'd expect. As a friend.

DARREN: Hang on…

LOGAN: As a *loyal friend*…I mean that's the etiquette here, right? That's the *code*. You'd choose me over her.

DARREN: …you're *asking* me to evict her?

LOGAN: Not gonna be easy to find somewhere now.

DARREN: Jesus…

LOGAN: Not in London. Not for that money…

DARREN: Logan…look…

LOGAN: In fact. *(Gets his phone out and dials.)* …you're gonna make her homeless, you'd better do it quick, yeah, give her time to get her shit together.

DARREN: What are you doing?

LOGAN places the phone on the table and on loudspeaker as it rings through.

LOGAN: It's the humane thing to do, ok? Fast. Bullet to the head.

DARREN: Fucking hell Logan.

MARTHA: *(On phone.)* Hello?

LOGAN: Oh hey Martha I'm sitting here with Darren.

MARTHA: *(On phone.)* Right.

LOGAN: Say hello Daz. Go on.

DARREN: H…hi…ya.

MARTHA: *(On phone.) Hi…(?)*

LOGAN: Darren's got something urgent he wants to talk to you about. Take it away Daz.

DARREN is glaring savagely at LOGAN.

LOGAN: Well go on.

DARREN: Shit. You…Uh. Hi Martha…you all right?

MARTHA: *(On phone.)* What's so urgent Darren? Is everything ok?

DARREN rubs his face in agony.

DARREN: Yeah. No. Great. Actually. Uh…but listen…

LOGAN: What Darren's trying to tell you Martha…

DARREN: Don't! Jesus!

67

LOGAN: Is we think we should all get together for dinner. The four of us.

MARTHA: *(On phone.)* Dinner?

LOGAN: Why not? Saturday night? At ours. OK?

MARTHA: *(On phone.)* O...ok...

LOGAN: Great. See you Saturday!

LOGAN hangs up. Grins at DARREN.

LOGAN: Your face.

LOGAN drinks. DARREN glares. Bell rings.

GAME TWELVE – AFTER DINNER SECRETS

MARTHA, JENNY and LOGAN are sitting in a circle. DARREN hands out paper and pens. They have all been drinking and we are well into the evening.

DARREN: So this is the game. Paper and pens.

MARTHA: Oh God Darren not another one of your puerile games.

JENNY: I like a party game.

DARREN: Thank you Jenny.

LOGAN: Will we have to do a lot of writing? I'm not really in a fit state.

DARREN: I'm sure you'll manage. So everyone has to write down some dirty little secret. Anonymously. We read it out, vote for whose secret we think it is.

MARTHA: Do we ever find out who actually wrote it?

DARREN: You never own up, no.

JENNY: Can it be about anything?

DARREN: Long as it's interesting Jenny.

MARTHA: I can't think of anything interesting.

LOGAN: Make it up.

JENNY: For God's sake, doesn't that totally defeat the point of the game.

LOGAN: Sorry?

DARREN: Jenny's right. It should be real. It should also be dark, shady, you know, embarrassing. Stuff you'd never admit to in public.

LOGAN: Jesus Dazzle, that's a bit much.

JENNY: It's got to have an element of shock? Is that right Darren?

DARREN: That's exactly right Jenny, yes. Or filth.

JENNY: I love this.

MARTHA: I really don't have anything filthy. Or shocking.

DARREN: Well any secret then. Anything embarrassing.

MARTHA: But I tell Logan everything.

JENNY: That's interesting.

MARTHA: Or my Nan.

JENNY: Logan. Do you tell Martha all *your* secrets?

LOGAN: Jesus Christ...

JENNY: Cos you're pretty tight lipped with me.

MARTHA: Well, no, no it's just, I think he feels, with me, you know, *safe*.

JENNY: Oh. Safe? And he doesn't feel safe with me?

MARTHA: Oh no I didn't mean...

JENNY: I see, so I'm basically some sort of enemy?

LOGAN: Come on Jenny she didn't mean that...

DARREN: Ok. Ok. Ok. Ok. Time out guys. Time out. Yeah?

LOGAN: Martha and I, we've known each other since school, there're no surprises.

JENNY: Really? No surprises? Maybe you should write each other's secrets.

LOGAN: Christ…

MARTHA: Can we do that?

DARREN: That's not really the game…

LOGAN: Can we just do this. Yes? I mean if we're doing this can we just…

MARTHA: Fine.

LOGAN: Ok?

JENNY: Fine.

DARREN: Great. OK now everyone: finish writing their secret.

They write, ponder, finish writing.

DARREN: Now stick them in this hat and I'll shuffle 'em.

Everyone drops their papers in the hat except MARTHA.

LOGAN: Come on Martha.

MARTHA: Mine's really boring. Can I change it.

ALL: No!

MARTHA drops her paper into the hat.

DARREN: Now. We shimmy them about a bit. And then we pick one.

DARREN picks a slip of paper out of the hat.

LOGAN: Then what?

JENNY: Then we all have to decide who's secret it is. Am I right?

DARREN: Spot on, Jenny, that's bang on.

MARTHA: It's supposed to be anonymous yes?

DARREN: That's right.

MARTHA: What if people guess it's you?

LOGAN: You keep shtum.

DARREN: Yeah, you don't own up to it

JENNY: If she was better at keeping shtum she'd have more secrets.

LOGAN: I have a question? Why am I supposed to care?

JENNY: See what I have to live with? He's so torpid.

LOGAN: I teach games all day. This is a busman's holiday for me.

JENNY: What? Kicking balls and jumping about?

LOGAN: There's a little bit more to it than that.

JENNY: This is a game for adults. Not bozos. A game of the heart and mind. Isn't that right Darren?

DARREN: Well...

LOGAN: And at least my job's got some worth. Some *value*.

JENNY: Yeah cos no-one ever forgets their PE teacher do they? Always the most inspirational figure in any childhood!

MARTHA: Could you two shut up and let him read out the secret?

DARREN: Thank you Martha. Right. Ready? Here goes. "When I was twelve I shat on our neighbour's lawn and blamed their Jack Russell, Nigel."

Everyone hoots.

LOGAN: Darren you dirty fucker.

DARREN: My hands are clean mate.

JENNY: The dog was called *Nigel*?

MARTHA: *(Laughing.)* That is actually the kind of thing he'd do.

DARREN: Excuse me?

JENNY: Well it certainly wasn't me.

DARREN: Hang on, how come you're all ganging up on me? Logan's the one with no control over his motions.

JENNY: What?

MARTHA: Oh yes! Yes, that's true. You're always dashing for the loo at the worst times. What about that play we went to see?

DARREN: *Play*? Logan?

MARTHA: What was it called?

LOGAN: I blank out all plays.

MARTHA: …we were sitting right in the middle of the row and this one here's all oh God my bladder's fit to bursting! … And I said…

JENNY: Yeah, so are we gonna take a vote on this now or what? What's happening?

LOGAN: Yes. Let's get this over with. Please.

DARREN: Right, so you're all gonna say it was me.

LOGAN: You don't know that. We might surprise you.

MARTHA: Yeah. Don't judge us by your own low standards.

JENNY: We might have been bluffing.

73

DARREN: Fine. Hands up who thinks it was me.

Everyone but DARREN puts their hands up.

DARREN: Fine. I shat on my neighbour's lawn then. Ha ha.
But I didn't.

ALL: You did. *(Laughter.)*

DARREN: Next secret. *(Darren puts his hand in the hat and pulls
out another slip of paper.)* Oh you bastard. Logan. I know
you wrote this. Very funny.

LOGAN: Moi

DARREN: "I cried…" Jesus Logan.

LOGAN: Read it out then.

DARREN: "I cried," fine. Shut up and listen then. "I cried
when me and my parents came up to uni to surprise my
girlfriend and caught her shagging my flat mate." And it's
"my parents and I" you ill-educated dick-wad.

LOGAN: *(Laughing.)* My hands are clean mate.

MARTHA: Did your uni girlfriend really do that?

DARREN: That was a long time ago. The old Darren.

LOGAN: Yeah before he mutated into Wham.

JENNY: Wham?

MARTHA: And your parents were there? God.

DARREN: Mum and *step* dad actually and it's really not a very
interesting story shall we move on?

LOGAN: No, no, no, let's explore this a minute. Let's examine
this.

DARREN: I can hardly remember it…

LOGAN: Daz was seeing this drama student called Naomi Catford…

DARREN: Nina Crawford. And she did music theory.

JENNY: She sounds like a total strumpet.

LOGAN: Let's just say our boy here was smitten. Properly head over heels.

MARTHA: Oh no. Poor Darren.

DARREN: I'm completely fine. I'm absolutely fine.

LOGAN: Even considered marriage, didn't you mate?

DARREN: Enjoying this are you Logan?

LOGAN: Wanted his parents to meet her, his future bride, it's only natural.

DARREN: Mum and *step*-dad.

MARTHA: This is awful.

LOGAN: Decided to surprise her by coming up to uni a day earlier than planned.

JENNY: Logan, that's enough now…

LOGAN: Knew she was there because she was in some play…

DARREN: Concert. Handle's Messiah. Get your facts right if you're gonna do this, shithead…

LOGAN: Spends the whole journey up waxing lyrical about how special she is, how she's "the one", his future bride. Even made his dad stop at the service station so Dazzler here could buy a dozen roses.

DARREN: *Step*-dad.

JENNY: Jesus.

MARTHA: Oh this is too, too awful…

LOGAN: Anyway they get to the house. Park up. Creep into the hall, up the stairs…Mum, Step Dad Phil…Dazza holding his beautifully heartfelt bouquet…

JENNY: Stop milking it for Christ's sake.

LOGAN: They open the bedroom door and there's Nina. On all fours. Taking up the rear from Roger the Lodger and screaming for more.

LOGAN laughs. He is the only one. DARREN's shoulders have slumped. JENNY and MARTHA rush over to console DARREN.

MARTHA: Poor you, are you ok?

JENNY: That complete bitch.

DARREN: I don't…

MARTHA: You must have been mortified.

DARREN: Long time ago. So…

JENNY: I guarantee she had behavioural problems. You're well shot.

LOGAN: Why're you making a fuss of him? You're supposed to be mocking him. Isn't that point of the game?

JENNY: Shut up Logan. You and your idiot games.

LOGAN: *My* game?

MARTHA: Jenny's right. That was a real dick move.

JENNY: Are you able to go on with it Darren love?

DARREN: Sure. I'm a soldier. The show must go on.

LOGAN: Oh Jesus give me a break.

DARREN: Ok then. Pressing on with the game. *(Pulls another slip of paper out of the hat.) What we got? (Reads.)* "I have a" oh, ok, uhm, awkward...

LOGAN: Come on then. Do your worst. Read it out.

DARREN: *(He looks at MARTHA then at JENNY.)* Maybe I'll do another one.

LOGAN: No you bloody won't, you'll do that one.

DARREN: Seriously, Logan.

LOGAN: Read it out. We all want to hear it. Don't we?

MARTHA: Not really.

JENNY: I'm actually getting quite bored of this game.

LOGAN: Oh really? Really? Well I have to say I for one am *greatly* warming to it. Read it out Darren. Or are you too chicken?

DARREN: Ok. Fine. If you're so desperate for it. Here goes. *(Clears his throat and reads.)* "I have fallen in love with my best friend."

A stunned silence. The mood suddenly darkens.

LOGAN: This is a bollocks game.

DARREN: Oh ho ho ho...no you don't.

LOGAN: Let's move on.

DARREN: I thought you were greatly warming to it.

LOGAN: It's fucking naff. We're not five years old.

MARTHA: What's going on Logan?

LOGAN: You know I wouldn't write that.

MARTHA: What does that mean?

77

JENNY: Yes Logan, what *does* that mean?

Beat. LOGAN has no answer.

DARREN: Time to vote! Who thinks that's Logan's secret?

DARREN puts his hand up. Looks at the others.

DARREN: Jenny?

LOGAN: You prick.

JENNY puts her hand up. LOGAN stares at her. She stares back.

DARREN: Martha?

MARTHA looks at LOGAN. Studies his face. MARTHA looks at JENNY. Then back again at LOGAN.

Beat.

Suddenly LOGAN throws himself at DARREN. They form a crab-like wrestling position. LOGAN pins DARREN to the ground.

JENNY: What are they doing?

MARTHA: Boston Crab.

LOGAN: Yield!

DARREN: This what you mean by being in love with your best friend?

LOGAN: Fuck off, you're not my best friend.

JENNY: Who is then Logan?

LOGAN: *(Stops. Awkward. Looks up.) This is bullshit. (Storms out.)*

DARREN: I think we can both agree… *(Gasping for breath.)*…I won that. Can I use your bog Jenny?

JENNY: Upstairs, first on the right.

DARREN exits. MARTHA and JENNY are alone. They smile awkwardly. Silence.

MARTHA: Lovely stew.

JENNY: Thanks.

MARTHA: Did you use…in the…

JENNY: Star anise…Yes.

MARTHA: Right.

Awkward pause.

JENNY: Another drink.

MARTHA: No… thanks… but don't let me stop you…

JENNY: I'm ok. Thanks.

MARTHA smiles awkwardly. JENNY smiles awkwardly.

MARTHA: We should do this again.

JENNY: Yes.

MARTHA: Come to ours.

JENNY: We should.

MARTHA: Darren's actually…underneath all that.

JENNY: Yes, he seems…under all that…

MARTHA: Yes. I think he really is.

Beat.

JENNY: It's not awkward then?

MARTHA: Awkward?

JENNY: I mean under the circumstances.

MARTHA: I don't…

JENNY: Oh surely you can see he's got a crush on you?

MARTHA: Darren?!

JENNY: Oh come on Martha.

MARTHA: I really think you've misread that…

JENNY: If you say so…

MARTHA: I think what you're reading is his compulsion to flirt with every woman he sees. Thinks of himself as some kind of seduction machine.

JENNY: Never tried to seduce me.

MARTHA: Right, no, probably too terrified.

JENNY: Oh? Am I so horribly frightening?

MARTHA: Oh no, I didn't mean. God, no. Sorry, I meant cos you're…

JENNY: Off limits?

MARTHA: Exactly.

JENNY: That's noble of him.

MARTHA: …he even tried to give me seduction advice.

JENNY: Huh. To use on whom?

MARTHA: Someone at work. I'm not gonna do it.

JENNY: Why not?

MARTHA: …I…

JENNY: Probably feel you need to run it by Logan first. Get his seal of approval. Is that it?

Beat. MARTHA smiles awkwardly. JENNY stares at MARTHA, hard.

MARTHA: Maybe I will have some more wine.

JENNY pours a large glass of wine, glaring at MARTHA all the time. MARTHA takes the wine and drinks deeply.

MARTHA: You not having?

JENNY: Better not.

MARTHA frowns, drinks. JENNY watches MARTHA like a hawk. Silence. Finally…

MARTHA: I think if he wanted to sleep with me, he's had every opportunity.

JENNY looks at her wild with fury.

MARTHA: …I mean Darren.

JENNY: Oh. I know…

MARTHA: Me and Logan…honestly… you mustn't be worried about that.

JENNY: I'm really not love.

MARTHA: I mean…ok, yes…he tells me every stupid thing that passes through his skull, yes, and, yes, maybe he's a bit more…*guarded* with you…

JENNY: Oh look no. Ignore me. My hormones are a bit all over the place at the moment. That's all it is. It's fine.

MARTHA: Your…

JENNY: Honestly, forget it.

JENNY smiles. MARTHA searches her face…

MARTHA: Jenny are you…?

JENNY: Oh God, I'm so sorry. I was sure Logan would've told you.

MARTHA: No, he...

JENNY: We've been telling only close friends and relatives. Really. I just took it for granted, you two being so...

MARTHA: He hasn't said a word.

JENNY: I'm such a blabbermouth...

MARTHA: No, but it's wonderful. Congratulations.

JENNY: Oh God no, I didn't mean to offend you. I'm such a clumsy bitch.

MARTHA: You haven't.

JENNY: Probably Logan wanted to tell you in his own time.

MARTHA: Seriously. I'm really happy for you.

JENNY: Good. Because I'd really like us to be friends.

MARTHA: Me too.

JENNY: Great.

Awkward pause.

MARTHA: How far gone are you?

JENNY: Three and half months.

MARTHA: You can hardly tell.

JENNY: It's genetic. All the Sanchez women are the same... then our bellies just ping back into shape. You probably hate me.

MARTHA: No it's brilliant...really...

Awkward pause.

JENNY: Will you do me a favour?

MARTHA: Ok...

JENNY: ...will you...will you please not mention to Logan I told you.

MARTHA: No, no, I won't say a word...

JENNY: Swear it.

MARTHA: I swear.

JENNY: On the baby's life.

Beat.

MARTHA: On...

JENNY: He'll be so furious I blurted it out...

MARTHA: Jenny...

JENNY: Then I'd feel safe.

MARTHA: OK. I swear.

JENNY: On the baby's life?

MARTHA: On the baby's life.

JENNY: Thank you. Now we've got our own little secret.

JENNY smiles.

MARTHA smiles dubiously.

Bell rings.

GAME THIRTEEN – QUESTIONS

DARREN, JENNY, MARTHA and LOGAN address the audience.

DARREN: What would I say to my Dad if I met him now?

LOGAN: What's there to say?

MARTHA: Oh…uhm…I don't know.

JENNY: God, so many things. First. Why did you leave? No. Not that.

DARREN: I'd say. Hey Dad. Remember me?

MARTHA: We talk on FaceTime. Mum tends to police those conversations.

DARREN: I told you, I keep things positive. Keep moving, keep things fluid, I'm an emotional Beduin.

JENNY: When he walked out, Mum barely even reacted. "Santiago is on a new stage in the journey of his life."

LOGAN: What would I ask?

MARTHA: Otherwise it's long silences until he goes; "d'you want your mum?"

DARREN: Can't even remember his voice.

LOGAN: Can't see his face anymore. Close my eyes…nothing.

JENNY: One day I went down to that workshop took his hammer and laid into that boat. Jenny. Smashed it up.

MARTHA: So we're in this art gallery…

Bell rings. Art Gallery – LOGAN and MARTHA look at a large canvass in silence. MARTHA simmers with quiet rage. After a long silence …

LOGAN: "Las Meninas".

84

MARTHA seethes.

LOGAN: *(Over-pronouncing the Z as 'thhh'.)* Velas-*quez.*

MARTHA: Uhuh.

LOGAN: Bet I know what you like about this painting.

MARTHA: Why? Because you know me so well?

LOGAN: It's the way he puts himself into it. That's the artist. Did you know that? It's kind of self portrait.

MARTHA: Yes.

LOGAN: I mean look at him, he's showing us a scene of him *painting the scene.* He's inventing post-modernism hundreds of years before... Martha: Yup.

LOGAN: ...do you see? Way he exposes himself...way he looks right at you, like he's caught you out? Gives you the chills, right?

MARTHA: Hmm, I think it's very interesting you should use words like "exposed". Like "caught out".

LOGAN: Is it?

MARTHA: Are you feeling particularly guilty about something?

LOGAN: What?

MARTHA: Let's play a game. We're only allowed to speak in questions.

LOGAN: Why?

MARTHA: Don't you think we should draw some boundaries around this relationship?

LOGAN: Not really.

MARTHA: As a question. How would you define our relationship?

LOGAN: …I dunno, we have a laugh…

MARTHA: As a question.

LOGAN: Don't we have a laugh?

MARTHA: Actually, no, we don't. If you think about it, we hardly ever laugh…

LOGAN: Martha…

MARTHA: My turn. Do you think you'll marry Jenny?

LOGAN: What? I don't…what that's got to do with anything?

MARTHA: Isn't she's an important part of your life?

LOGAN: Yeah but why bring up marriage?

MARTHA: Don't you think it'd be appropriate under the circumstances?

LOGAN: What circumstances? What did she say to you?

MARTHA: Why can't you just be honest with me?

LOGAN: Has Jenny said something to you?

MARTHA: Don't you think we should finish this now?

LOGAN: Please God yes. I hate this game.

MARTHA: I mean this friendship.

She goes. LOGAN looks bemused.

Bell rings.

GAME FOURTEEN – READY OR NOT, HERE I COME

JENNY is beavering away at her laptop, when LOGAN enters. He stands there watching her for a moment, glaring at her, seething. She is oblivious.

LOGAN: I wanna talk to you.

JENNY: … hiya, sorry I'm on this really tight deadline…

LOGAN: It's important.

JENNY: So is this.

LOGAN: Jenny…

JENNY: Felix is launching his web site next week and I absolutely *must* finish these designs by tonight.

LOGAN: Oh well we mustn't upset Felix.

JENNY: …twenty minutes, I promise, we'll chat, ok, there's cold pizza in the fridge.

LOGAN: What did you say to Martha?

JENNY: *Martha*?

LOGAN: Why's she behaving like I'm a total stranger.

JENNY: How the hell would I know?

LOGAN: Jenny…

JENNY: I can't be responsible for whatever madness is going on in that frantic, muddled brain of hers? Now please I really need to do this.

LOGAN: You said something to her. Didn't you?

JENNY: I…

LOGAN: You talked to her the other night. After dinner. You *told* her something.

JENNY suddenly snaps her laptop shut, gets up and paces frantically.

JENNY: Fuck. Fuck. Fuck. I knew that little bitch would blab.

LOGAN: *Blab*?

JENNY: She swore to me, she swore it. On the life of our unborn child.

LOGAN: Our *what*?!

JENNY: ...that's the sort of *character* your precious Martha is. Treacherous. *Untrustworthy.* Breaking solemn oaths at the first sign of trouble...

LOGAN: ...just a minute...

JENNY: Cursed the embryonic little fucker without the slightest qualm.

LOGAN: What unborn child?

JENNY: What?

LOGAN: What unborn child? What the fuck're you talking about?

JENNY: She...but you said...

LOGAN: God now it makes sense.

JENNY: I...no...wait...

LOGAN: You told her you were pregnant? Christ.

JENNY: OK. It sounds bad...I know...

LOGAN: Why would you do that?

JENNY: I didn't actually *say* that...

LOGAN: This is really sick. You've done some really *sick* things recently but this...

JENNY: ...two of you are so fucking tight, so fucking exclusive, can you blame me for fighting dirty?

LOGAN: Well it worked, she wants no more to do with me. Congratulations.

JENNY: You should be thanking me.

LOGAN: What?

JENNY: ...you should be thanking me for freeing you from her. You used her as a crutch. You let her hold you back.

LOGAN: Hold me back?

JENNY: Yes.

LOGAN: From what?

JENNY: *From me! From giving yourself to me!* I see her looking at you, eyes shining, full of light, and all I can think about is squashing it.

LOGAN: You're gonna talk to her.

JENNY: You never took me to a Velasquez exhibition.

LOGAN: You're gonna tell her you were lying.

JENNY: You know she'll be a crap shag. She'll just lie there like an apple being cored.

LOGAN: At least she won't shriek. Like an eel being skinned.

JENNY: If you were any kind of man you already would, you'd have fucked her into next Tuesday by now, but you're not. Are you? You're emotionally stunted. Just like your fucking dad.

Suddenly and with terrible violence, LOGAN picks up the laptop and smashes down it on the floor. JENNY stares at it. A terrible silence descends.

LOGAN: Right. Shit. Sorry. Don't know where that came from.

JENNY: ...uhm...

LOGAN: I'll...look...

JENNY: Fuck.

LOGAN: ...I'll fix it...

JENNY: Fix it?

LOGAN: No. I'll...ok, I'll go to John Lewis...

JENNY: You'll...

LOGAN: Buy you another one I'll...

JENNY: It's gone. It's all fucking gone.

LOGAN: Didn't you back it up?

JENNY: No I was in the middle of...no.

LOGAN: Shit.

JENNY: If you break it, it's gone. Forever. You can't just...

LOGAN: I don't...

JENNY: Go to John Lewis.

LOGAN: I don't know what's happening to us.

Pause.

JENNY: But I worked so hard at this...

LOGAN: I can't lose her.

LOGAN exits. JENNY hangs her head. Bell rings.

GAME FIFTEEN – DEBRIEFING

Flat. DARREN is there when MARTHA enters. She stares at him. He grins.

DARREN: Hi.

MARTHA: Why? Why did I listen to you?

DARREN: I thought you were out with Logan tonight.

MARTHA: I left.

Her expression is bank, distant. Finally, she slumps on the couch.

DARREN: Martha, what happened?

MARTHA: I…

DARREN: Did he…

MARTHA: Hospital.

DARREN: Hospital?

MARTHA: Logan.

DARREN: Logan's in the hospital?

MARTHA: Dr…

DARREN: Martha…

MARTHA: …boner…

DARREN: What?

MARTHA: Oh God… so humiliating.

DARREN: For God's sake what? Did something happen with Logan?

MARTHA: *(Snapping.)* It's got fuck all to do with him?

DARREN: Ok.

MARTHA: I tried your stupid moves.

DARREN: Shit. That Dr. Boner. Brilliant. Tell all.

MARTHA: It was a nightmare.

DARREN: Why? Did you mess up the order of play? That's often where the rookies fall down.

MARTHA: It was mortifying. I made a total fool of myself. Ok?

DARREN: I insist you talk me through it. Blow by blow.

MARTHA: I don't want to do a bloody post mortem on it. It was a shambles of cosmic proportions, let's just leave it at that.

DARREN: Sorry. No can do. As your mentor It's crucial we go through a thorough debriefing.

MARTHA: I feel sick.

DARREN: Of the whole sorry episode. Or how will you improve for next time?

MARTHA: Next time?! You don't seem to understand. This was the worst thing that ever happened to anyone.

DARREN: I'm sure that's not true.

MARTHA: *(Violently.)* Are you? Were you there? No! So how could you possibly know that?

DARREN: Which is why I want you to describe it for me.

MARTHA: Christ Darren…

DARREN: And don't leave out any of the gruesome details.

MARTHA: …the thought of re-living that horror.

DARREN: This is the optimum time to do this. While you're still reeling, still such a pathetic wreck. Get it all out, get as low as you can get. It's cleansing.

MARTHA: *Cleansing?*

DARREN: Come on. From the top. Where'd it happen? What was the venue?

MARTHA: Oh God. Fine. In the canteen.

DARREN: Ok. Canteen, good, while he's relaxing. Good strategy.

MARTHA: I knew David had an evening shift, I know his schedule backwards.

DARREN: Planning. Excellent. Be informed about the target... Go on.

MARTHA: I found him sitting on his own and I thought this is my chance. I went over. Plomped myself down at the table across from him. I never plomp. I'm not a plomper.

DARREN: Oh plomping's the best. I'm a prolific plomper.

MARTHA: And that's when it comes out of my mouth. *(Swallows, then delivers it.)* "Hey Doctor Boner. I've got cling film and shit loads of lube. Wanna meet me in the stock room and we can slosh around like eels in a bucket?"

Pause.

DARREN: Oh God.

MARTHA: His jaw was hanging there. Practically swinging from side to side.

DARREN: You were supposed to tell Kenny about the lube.

MARTHA: It's so awful.

DARREN: Did everything I taught you just…fall out of your head or what?

MARTHA: Oh I can't bear it, I can't bear it.

DARREN: I knew it. What did I say about getting the order right? You don't kick off with lube. Rule number one.

MARTHA: I want to die. I want to crawl under and rock and…

DARREN: So. All right. All right. You blurted out about the lube. Is that it?

MARTHA: No, no, it gets worse. It gets so much worse. I look up and the whole table is surrounded. It was a bloody departmental dinner. They're all standing there. Everyone I work with, all the bosses too, they're standing there with…with their trays and their chilli con carne and their mouths on the floor, and then Lucy, Nurse Forbes, she says, "When you say Doctor Boner do you mean Dr Roberts?" And I say yeah it's just a fun nickname. And then David says: "Please don't call me that again." And I point at him and say *(She swallows.)* "This one's keen. Didn't your mother teach you not to interrupt?" Oh God.

DARREN: Ooh. You're carrying on the seduction?

MARTHA: Something was kicking in.

DARREN: That'll be the training.

MARTHA: It was all a blur, I couldn't stop myself.

DARREN: Yeah, I would have aborted at this point.

MARTHA: And then Mr. Chaterjee, he's the chief consultant, he's frowning and all stern and he goes "what's all this about lubricant? I hope you haven't been mishandling hospital property for your own private amusement Dr Roberts. We all like a little light-heartedness, but the stock room needs to be kept sanitary." And I go. "Don't interrupt. Didn't your mum ever beat you?!"

DARREN: To the consultant?

MARTHA: Yes!

DARREN: Why?!

MARTHA: I don't know, he's like seventy years old.

DARREN: Jesus Martha.

MARTHA: Then David, he starts stammering and says "I honestly don't know what she's talking about Mr. Chaterjee? In fact" he says…and this hit me like a train… "I hardly know this woman." God. It was shattering. In that moment I realised…I saw it so clearly…this whole time I'd been living a fantasy. I'd had so many imaginary conversations with him, I started to believe they were real.

DARREN: I don't know what to say.

MARTHA: Then I fainted.

DARREN: You fainted?!

MARTHA: Someone must have scooped me up and given me a sedative. I woke up on a gurney in Fenton Ward. I just want to forget it ever happened…

DARREN: This is my fault. I should never've let you go in-field so soon, you weren't ready.

MARTHA: You won't tell Logan about this.

DARREN: No, God no.

MARTHA: I'm such a colossal fuck up.

DARREN: Yes.

MARTHA: I repel men. Every relationship, I bollocks it up, I screw it up. *Spectacularly.*

DARREN: Oh you're a motorway pile-up, no sane person would argue. You want some tea? Or...

MARTHA: Actually could you just ...for a long time...not speak.

DARREN: Sure. Sure. No problem.

Long silence. MARTHA seems to be shivering. DARREN sits down and rubs her. She snuggles up to him. He strokes her hair. She settles back. He strokes her face. She touches his fingers. She looks at him. He looks at her. They draw closer together. Suddenly he stops. He jumps up.

MARTHA: What?

DARREN: Sorry this is...

MARTHA: Oh...

DARREN: Inappropriate, when you're...so... I don't want to...

MARTHA: Right.

DARREN: Not that...under normal circumstances... I wouldn't...you know...

MARTHA: Really?

Loud buzzing.

DARREN: Shit. I'd better...

DARREN goes. MARTHA paces. Checks herself in a mirror. Suddenly LOGAN storms in.

LOGAN: I want to talk to you Martha.

MARTHA: What is it, what d'you want?

96

DARREN enters.

LOGAN: Give us a minute Daz will you mate?

DARREN: Bit late in the day, old son.

LOGAN: Come on old chum make yourself scarce.

DARREN: I don't think so old bean.

MARTHA: What do you want Logan?

LOGAN: I want to speak to you. In private.

DARREN: Why don't you stop messing her about.

LOGAN: Excuse me?

DARREN: Can't you see how inappropriate this is?

LOGAN: What d'you know about it?

DARREN: I glean things.

LOGAN: Oh you glean things do you?

DARREN: Yes I glean things. I glean you've been using her…

LOGAN: Oh you glean that do you?

MARTHA: Stop it you two. Stop gleaning will you. God's sake.

DARREN: You've been stringing her along mate, and it's
    fucking dishonest.

LOGAN: Dishonest? You trick women into bed.

DARREN: But I never tricked anyone into putting their entire
    life on hold. That's just cruel mate.

LOGAN: I didn't do that. Did I ever do that? Martha.

MARTHA: I…

DARREN: You don't have to answer that Martha.

97

LOGAN: I want to know what the fuck it's got to do with you?

DARREN: Martha's under my tutelage now.

LOGAN: She's what?

MARTHA: Oh God.

LOGAN: Your tutelage?

DARREN: My stewardship, yes, so I'm gonna have to ask you to leave.

LOGAN: Piss off. I left Jenny.

MARTHA: You...

DARREN: That's irrelevant.

LOGAN: ...there's so much I want to talk to you about...

MARTHA: You can't leave a woman in that condition.

DARREN: What condition?

LOGAN: That's the thing. There is no condition.

MARTHA: Logan.

LOGAN: She's not pregnant. She made the whole thing up.

MARTHA: She...

LOGAN: She wanted to scare you off, drive a wedge between us.

MARTHA: Why?

DARREN: Easy. She's threatened by you.

LOGAN: Darren you don't know anything about this ok, so please...

MARTHA: Why would she be threatened by me?

DARREN: Because he's in love with you. Isn't it bloody obvious?

LOGAN: Ok. Will you please fuck off now?

MARTHA: Sorry. Hang on. Because he what?

LOGAN: She forced me to choose, Martha, and I chose you.

MARTHA looks stunned.

DARREN: Well you're too late. Sorry.

LOGAN: Excuse me.

DARREN: We had a moment just now. A real moment, so you can pack up your shitshow and move it out, buddy. It's my rodeo now.

LOGAN: Fuck you and your moment. Is this true?

MARTHA: Oh Jesus...

LOGAN: Is this a joke, some kind of horrific joke?

DARREN: Nothing either of us could do to stop it. Like an express train, like a driving inevitability, a primal lust.

LOGAN: No. No. You need to back off, son, back off.

DARREN: Why should I?

LOGAN: Because I saw her first!

MARTHA: What?

LOGAN: It's bad form and you know it. You went against the code.

MARTHA: Am I actually visible?

LOGAN: You went against the male loyalty code and you know it. And I want what's mine Darren, so do not...do *not do not* get in my way.

DARREN: And let you win? I don't think so.

LOGAN: Why not? I always do.

DARREN: You don't deserve her?

LOGAN: And *you* do?

DARREN: …least I didn't have her on the bench all these years.

LOGAN: You know fuck all about it.

DARREN: You foul things up with Jenny, suddenly Martha's being waved on to the pitch. Is that fair?

LOGAN: That's not how it is…

MARTHA: Uh…Can *I* speak?

DARREN: She's a consolation fuck, nothing more. The second you get your leg over, you'll slink off with your trousers round your ankles.

MARTHA: *Darren*?!

DARREN: You don't actually want to *be* with her.

LOGAN: Oh and you do?

DARREN: I've developed, yes, feelings. *Real* feelings.

LOGAN: That's funny, cos, that's interesting, cos when we spoke recently, about Martha, you were at pains to point out what a massive snob she was.

MARTHA: What?

LOGAN: What a snooty bitch she was, how she looked down her nose at you, made you feel *small*.

DARREN: Now wait a minute…

MARTHA: You said that about me?

DARREN: …that was…no…well yes but…

MARTHA: You called me a snooty bitch?

DARREN: Yes, no, yes, I… but I didn't mean…

MARTHA: I don't believe this …

LOGAN: Always moping about the house, whining about how she fancied Doctor David…

MARTHA: You told him?! Darren? You *told* him.

DARREN: I…I…Martha…

MARTHA: I trusted you.

DARREN: *(Furiously to Logan.)* I told you that in confidence you little prick.

LOGAN: You broke that covenant when you moved in my territory. I'm her soul mate. Ok? *Pal.* We're meant to be, always were. You're just passing through, you're a *footnote* in her life. I'm the destination.

Beat. Suddenly DARREN and LOGAN throw themselves into a long, silent wrestling match.

The wrestling gets vicious. LOGAN overwhelms DARREN, DARREN overwhelms LOGAN. It goes on, until, finally, they stop, look deeply into each other's eyes.

MARTHA grabs a soda streamer from the bar and sprays it at them.

They break apart howling from the cold water until they collapse in a heap, puffing and panting.

MARTHA: I'm *this close, this close* walking out that door and never speaking to either of you dickheads again.

LOGAN: Give me one night. One night. Let me show you.

MARTHA: We've been out a million times.

LOGAN: Exactly, I know everything about you.

DARREN: I put myself out there just now, made myself vulnerable for the first time in years and you...you brought that out of me, you inspired me Martha and now you have an *obligation* to finish this.

MARTHA: I've...

LOGAN: What?

DARREN: You have, yes, an *obligation* Martha. To finish what you started.

LOGAN: Ok it's up to you. Pick one of us.

MARTHA: What? How can you do that to me?

DARREN: Logan's absolutely right. You have to choose. Him or me.

MARTHA: How can you put me in this position?

LOGAN: There's no choice.

MARTHA: Ok. I'm going to talk now. I've thought about being with both of you. Actually. Thought seriously about it. Logan; there has, yes, always been, I suppose, something between us. When you stood up for me in class all those years ago, I think my heart burst for the first time and it's never been the same. You'll always have real meaning for me. And honestly in the last few months, a word from you a look, even, and I'd have been yours. Completely. And Darren. You're such a strange little man. In spite of all your babbling, I feel sort of *safe* with you. So many times I wanted to curl up with you...cocoon myself inside you, stay there for forever. And you've been looking out for me, I know that. You made me feel I could break out of myself. Be bold. Be someone totally new. And that moment we had just now...yes... maybe if Logan hadn't come over things might've gone differently. I was feeling so vulnerable I could've just…fallen into you. But this last few minutes you've sort of revealed something so… both of you…so…dysfunctional, I've got nowhere to turn. Making me choose? Well I've made my decision. For once, I'm not gonna take the screwed-up option. I'm not gonna go around in circles, I'm not gonna play this preposterous game anymore. I'm breaking the pattern. I'm leaving. *(Walks to the exit and turns, to address the others, holding her head up in an airily grand manner and with a lump in her throat.)* Goodbye then. I wish you both well in all your endeavours. I'll send for my things.

MARTHA exits.

LOGAN: *(Turns to Darren angrily jabbing his finger at him.)* Bell end!

Bell rings.

GAME SIXTEEN – HOT SEATING PART II

JENNY, DARREN, LOGAN and MARTHA address the audience.

JENNY: After Martha rejected him he came crawling back to me. Tail between his legs.

MARTHA: I thought it was very telling that he immediately ran back to Jenny.

LOGAN: Events had caused me to reconsider. To think about what she'd done and why.

MARTHA: I applied for another job. Near where my parents live.

DARREN: Sure, I broke down. Broke every one of my own rules. Lost my shit. But I don't regret it. I'm human. I'm flawed. But you get up off the floor, you reconstruct yourself, better this time. Tougher.

LOGAN: Darren is a tit.

DARREN: No me and Logan are not mates any more.

LOGAN: We grab the occasional beer.

DARREN: The odd game of squash, yeah but...

LOGAN: Sometimes I go around for a game on his X box.

DARREN: I'm pretty sure, when I'm not looking, he sniffs her bed.

JENNY: He always was a weirdo.

DARREN: What have I learned from all this? Good one. Key question...

LOGAN: I've learned fuck all. I do miss her though.

DARREN: I've learned; sometimes people can surprise you.

MARTHA: I've learnt sometimes you can surprise yourself.

DARREN: I've learned this too; pairing up. It's a primal need.

LOGAN: Things are actually going fine with Jenny.

DARREN: We built our society around it. We build our technology around it.

JENNY: Do I feel like second choice?

LOGAN: We still live together. It feels right.

JENNY: As long as I'm the last choice.

LOGAN: What I mean is… it doesn't feel wrong.

JENNY: But it feels…if I'm honest…

DARREN: It feels, doesn't it, like we're in the eye of a revolution, like we're at a cliff edge. Like we're all waiting…wondering…what next?

JENNY: Feels like he's half there.

DARREN: What next for the human species? Where do we go from here?

JENNY: But at least he's there.

MARTHA: *(As she talks the lights fade and the others recede.)* As I was leaving the hospital that last time, David came over. Asked what my plans were. Said…and this made me smile…that the "lube fiasco", as he called it, had become legendary. Become this story he told people, a party piece. Among his circle of friends, I'd been built up to become this mythical figure. Crazy Martha. He even confessed to feeling heady in my presence, nervy, that, now, confronted with the flesh-and-blood person, he suddenly had butterflies, and I realised…I had the power now. I laughed. Then…ever so slightly…I touched the nape of my neck…

END OF PLAY

WWW.OBERONBOOKS.COM